Hidden

Shadows

Linda's Story

Colleen Anne

Colleen Anne

ISBN 978-0-615-37339-3

This novel is a work of fiction. Names, characters, places, and incidents either are the product of the author's imagination or are used fictitiously, and any resemblance to actual persons living or dead, events, or locales is entirely coincidental.

Dedication

This book is dedicated to my family. A special thanks goes to Jerry Breen's daughters for all of their support.

Table of contents

INTRODUCTION

James Stealth had worked for the same company for over fifteen years. He and his wife Courtney lived in the same small house in the center of New York City where they were raising their two boys. Courtney was an author of children's books; she had been published many times and interviewed in many magazines, but they were not happy. Their love was growing deeper as their boys were growing bigger, but there was something missing.

It was the spring of 2009 when James came through the front door with news of his company was opening up a new business in upstate New York. That night he sat across the table from Courtney drinking his evening beer and said "This is a big change for us. Are you sure that you are ready for this?" he asked his wife.

"James, this is a chance for us to have a better life for the boys. You know I have always wanted to get a house in the country for them, a place where they can have a dog and a yard to play in. I can write books anywhere. Besides with your job, I don't even need to sell my work," she replied.

"Well then, I guess we just need to find a house," James replied.

Courtney jumped up from the table and ran to the boy's room. "Boys, we are moving and you will be able to have your own rooms."

The following week, James took a few days off to meet with the realtors in Salem. The pictures of the house were beautiful. The company that James worked for needed him to start the following week so there was no time to take a good look. "I assure you Mr. and Mrs. Stealth that this house is as beautiful in person as it is in the pictures," Jeremiah explained.

"We just showed the house last week to a couple and it is in excellent shape," stated his partner and wife Sadie.

Jeremiah and Sadie were an elderly couple who should have retired years ago. Jeremiah was in his eighties with gray hair, well what was left was gray, and he was about one hundred and fifty pounds with an arch in his back. Sadie, on the other hand, was about seventy with a full head of gray wavy shoulder length hair. She had beautiful skin, the kind that you only see on models in their twenties. She stood about five feet tall and talked with a quiet, almost calming voice. The pair of them showed the kind of love for each other that you only dreamed you could have after fifty plus years of marriage. "What do you think James?" Courtney asked.

"It is up to you Hon, I love it, but you are the one who will be home most of the time. So what do you think?"James replied.

"I love it!" She yelled excitedly and the Stealth's signed the papers and had purchased their first country home. The home they hoped to raise their family and grow old together in. Only time and the secrets of the house will tell whether James and Courtney will get that chance.

CHAPTER

ONE

WELCOME HOME

James Stephen, and Courtney Jean, Stealth arrived at their new home at thirty four Beacon Road in Salem, New York. Their boys, Andy, and Billy were already out of the truck and on the front porch waiting for their parents to open the door. Billy was holding their cat Mako, in his arms.

Courtney got out of the passenger side of the truck with a huge smile on her face, turned, looked and waited for James. James and Courtney walked hand in hand onto the porch of the old farm style house and James unlocked the front door. Billy put Mako on the living room carpet and then Andy and Billy tore up the stairs pushing and shoving each other as they both wanted to make sure they got the perfect room. Courtney turned to James before they even walked in, and kissed him on the cheek. "Welcome home," she said then walked through the front door. They could hear the moving truck pull into the drive way.

"The truck is here C.J. I will go talk to them," James said. Then James kissed his wife and walked back out toward the driveway.

Courtney was standing in the living room. She picked up the cat and she looked around, took a deep breath and walked farther into the house. She could see the spot over the fireplace that she and James planned on putting the family portrait. She then turned her attention to the dining room where she could almost picture the family eating dinner right now. She proceeded into the kitchen where she had forgotten that there was a dishwasher until she saw it. She then turned and went into the bathroom and said to herself "I still can't believe this is ours," as she patted the cat on the head. "This house is too good to be true," she said as she could hear the boys laughing and carrying on upstairs. The sound of their laughter brought a smile to Courtney's face.

Courtney then walked back out to the living room and looked out the window. She could see the pool in the yard and the large oak tree that James was going to put the tire swing on. She could also see the swing set waiting for her children to play on it and the club house the boys already played in when they first looked at the house. She walked to the stairs and listened to the boys talking about the rooms that they had picked.

James came back in the front door. "The guys are going to start bring the furniture in C.J. Just tell them where to put things because I have no clue where you want stuff," James told Courtney with a slight laugh in his voice.

"Okay, I think I can handle that. Most of the boxes are labeled what room anyway," she replied as she put Mako in the downstairs bathroom and shut the door. Being an indoor cat, Courtney was scared he may run out and get lost.

The movers began bringing in the furniture, first starting with the boys things. They were careful not to damage the walls as they were going up the stairs. Courtney could hear the boys telling the movers where to put their belongings. She thought she should go up and make sure that things were going well.

Courtney was at the top of the stairs in the doorway to what was now Andy's room. She was watching as Andy was telling the man to put his bed on the wall that faced the back of the house and his dresser on the left wall. She found it funny that her twelve year old thought that he was in charge. She then walked into Billy's room and watched as he jumped on the bed that they had already put in place. Billy, being nine, thought this was the most fun ever, but Courtney told him he needed to stop jumping before he got hurt. As she walked toward her bedroom she glanced into the boy's toy room that was next to Billy's room to see all the boxes that would need to be unpacked. Then she continued into her and James' room that was across the hall on the right. There was no furniture in this room yet. She walked over to the small room that was attached to it. She remembered the realtor telling her that this was the nursery. Courtney and James had already talked about this becoming their office that Courtney would be working from.

Courtney looked up over her head and saw the drop downstairs that led to the attic. She walked over and pulled the string to the stairs. She climbed the stairs as far as she needed to just take a quick look. She could see old furniture covered in sheets and cob webs everywhere. She glanced behind her and let out a scream when she saw a huge spider, and just about fell coming down the ladder. She closed the stairs back up and said to herself. "I'm not going back up there without James. That spider was creepy." Then she walked back out into the bedroom and looked out the window. She could see the garage that James had already said needed a new paint job. She then walked back to the bedroom door and watched the movers bring the last of the boxes into Billy's room. She knew that her room was going to be next. She smiled as she saw James round the corner from the stairway. "I was going to check out the attic and I noticed a bunch of furniture, but there was a huge spider, so I changed my mind," she said with a little giggle and kissed her husband.

The two of them were in the bedroom showing the movers where to put stuff. They then went downstairs to make sure they moved the rest of the furniture and boxes where they wanted them. When the movers were gone, Courtney and James sat on their couch and put their feet on the coffee table. Courtney was curled up in James' arms just listening to the boys unpack their rooms. Courtney got up after what seemed to be hours. She knew that she needed to get the boys to come down and get washed up for dinner. She had already ordered the pizza. "Boys dinner will be here soon, come and get washed up," she said.

Courtney went into the kitchen. She had to find the box with the paper plates. She got them out to set the table, and even though it was just pizza, it was their first meal in the house, their new home. She wanted everything to be perfect. She came back out into the dining room and set the table. She watched as James paid for the pizza smiling, thinking things were finally looking good for her family. They all gathered at the table and ate.

Courtney watched as the boys talked about their new rooms and what they were going to be doing to them, how they were setting things up. They had never had their own rooms. She then looked at James and for the first time in a long time, he looked happy. That is something he had lost a long time ago. It was nice to see it come back.

Courtney was clearing the table and she could hear the boys

playing in the yard. James was on the couch watching the weather channel. She shook her head in amazement and thought about how lucky she was. These are the best boys and James, James is the most wonderful man on the planet. She then took a deep breath. She walked back into the living room to see that the boys were curled up on the floor laying on pillows covered up with a blanket watching cartoons. James was on the couch sleeping. Courtney smiled and sat down in the chair. She wanted to have a fire in the fireplace, but it was summertime and she did not want it to be too hot for the kids.

Courtney and James awoke at six am that next morning. James needed to get ready for work. It was Tuesday and it was summer vacation for the kids so Courtney let the boys sleep in. She got up because she wanted to say goodbye to James and get a few things unpacked before the boys were up for the day. She got James' lunch ready and walked him to the front door, kissed him goodbye and closed the front door behind him. She looked around and saw that there was a lot to get done. She decided to start in the kitchen. She grabbed a steak knife off the kitchen table and used it to slice open the box that contained the crock pot and coffee pot and a few other kitchen items. She worked for a few hours and got the whole kitchen unpacked and put away. She was just getting ready to get started on the dining room when Billy walked down the stairs. "Morning, Mommy," he stated and walked over to Courtney, rubbing his eyes.

"Morning, Hon. How did you sleep in your new room?" she asked as she hugged him and kissed him on the forehead.

"I slept great! I love having my own room," he said as he walked to the refrigerator and got out the milk. Courtney got the cereal down from the cabinet and got out a bowl. She smiled as Billy took the cereal and poured it into the bowl. She thought to herself about how independent he was becoming. She saw out of the corner of her eye that Andy was walking through the living room and entered the kitchen. "Good morning, Andy, how was your first night here? She asked as she walked over and kissed his forehead.

"I slept good Mom. I like it here. There are no sounds of cars going by at night," he said as she got him out a bowl and a spoon. She sat with a cup of tea while the boys ate there breakfast.

Once they were finished, they went into the living room and watched cartoons while Courtney unpacked the dining room dishes and put them in the hutch. She put the antique table cloth that her Nana gave her on the table and hung up all the pictures of the family and took a deep breath, smiled, and headed to the living room. She walked in to see the boys curled up on the couch with the cat sleeping between them. She could see they were watching Sponge Bob Square Pants. She shook her head and giggled a bit because she hated that show. She opened the box that was on the coffee table and started hanging the pictures and putting the knickknacks on the end tables next to the couch. She then took the family portrait out of the box and hung it over the mantel and took a step back to make sure that it was straight. She brought another box down and went through it. This contained the wedding album and other albums of the family over the years.

Courtney put all the albums on the top shelf of the wooden video rack. She was so proud of her family pictures and shared them with anyone who would look at them. She then took out the videos and loaded them on the shelf, then took the empty boxes out to the porch. Feeling a bit tired, she sat in the chair in the living room. The boys were now upstairs in there playroom and she could hear the video game they were playing. She put the kicker back on the chair and Mako jumped up on her lap. She grabbed the remote and watched the weather channel as she wanted to take the boys to the creek that ran behind the house. She was petting Mako's long gray fur when she noticed he had bumps down his side. She wasn't sure what she was feeling so she parted his hair with her hands and noticed scratches down his sides. Knowing he was not outside of the house, she wondered how he got them. "Boys!" she called. Andy and Billy came running down the stairs.

"What, Mom?" Andy asked with Billy right next to him.

"Do you guys have any idea what happened to the cat?" she asked. "He has scratches down his sides," she said.

"I have no clue Mom," Billy stated.

"Me either," Andy added. "I heard him cry out last night, but I am not sure why," Andy then added.

"Well, we have to keep an eye on him. He may have gotten stuck some place with all the boxes being unpacked. Just keep a closer eye out for him, okay?" she said as she got up and put the cat back in the chair and patted his head. "I wanted to take you guys to the creek out back to swim. Are you interested?" Courtney asked. Of course both boys were excited. Courtney told them to go get their suits on and she then went into the kitchen to get some sandwiches for a picnic near the water. She yelled to the boys "Grab towels please." When the lunch was packed and the boys were ready, the three of them left the house.

Courtney and the boys walked down the path at the edge of the property to the creek that was fed by a lake that was nearby. The boys were excited and ran ahead. "Don't get in that water until I get there!" Courtney yelled. She could hear a little girl laughing as she walked toward the water. She looked around, but could not see anyone. She continued down the path until she got to the water. The boys waited for their mom to get settled in on a grassy spot where she laid out a blanket to sit. "Okay boys, you can get in now," she said as she got her book out of the bag she had their lunches in. Courtney opened the book she was reading as the boys swam. She was a science fiction lover. She was deep into a book called "Bugged." It caught her attention on the bookshelf at Barnes and Nobles because it was by a new author.

The boys finished their swim then came and sat on the blanket. They were both in a towel. Courtney got out their sandwiches and juice boxes. She put her book away and chatted with the boys about the house and the yard and how it will be to start a new school in the fall. When they were finished with their lunch, they walked back toward the house. Courtney could hear laughter again in the distance. "Do you guys hear that?" she asked.

"No, Mom," Billy said. "Can't hear anything unless you mean the water."

"Never mind I guess I am just hearing things," she said in return and kept walking. When they got back in the yard, Andy stopped at the swing set and hopped on. Courtney pushed him for a few minutes while Billy ran around the yard kicking a ball. They were so happy to finally have a yard to play in. The place that they rented in the city had no place for the boys to play. Courtney and James would take them to the park often, but it was not the same as a yard of their own to play in.

When Andy was finished swinging, the three of them headed back into the house. Billy and Andy headed upstairs to finish unpacking the toys in their toy room. Courtney put the towels in the drier and tossed out their garbage from lunch. She then yelled to the boys to take off their bathing suits and throw them down so she could wash them. With the suits washing with the laundry from last night, Courtney started dinner. She seasoned the roast and then covered it and put it in the oven and turned and left the kitchen. She sat on the couch and watched television for a littlewhile. Realizing there was nothing good on; she decided to go join the kids in the toy room. The boys had all the boxes unpacked and were putting the toys away. She told them they were doing a good job and took the empty boxes out to the porch. She then checked on Mako who was still sleeping in the chair. She could see that he was comfortable so she did not want to disturb him. She walked back upstairs to the toy room. "I'm going to get in the shower while dinner is cooking, so behave boys," she said.

"We will," the boys said at almost the same time. Then Courtney went into the bathroom and turned on the shower. She was looking around to see where she could put all her dolphin figurines and she could picture the wallpaper border she had already picked out. In her mind she could see the dolphins on the walls and blue paint she and James had planned on putting up this weekend.

Courtney got her clothes and got in the shower. When she was finished, she put her robe on and went to check on the boys. She then continued to the bedroom and got dressed. Then Courtney walked through the bedroom and into the office. She looked at the desk and knew she had a lot of unpacking to do. She shook her head and left the office. "I will deal with that room tomorrow," she said to herself as she walked back out her bedroom door. She went downstairs and went into the kitchen and got out the dinner dishes. She took them into the dining room and set them on the table. She then sat on the couch in the living room and turned the television on. She watched a few talk shows as the kids played upstairs.

Courtney finished watching television and set the table just as James had come in from work. "How was your day?" she said as she kissed her husband on the cheek.

"It was good, nothing really to talk about. What's for dinner? I am starving," he said as he sat at the dinner table.

"I made a roast," Courtney said and called the boys down for dinner.

The family sat at the table and enjoyed their dinner. She explained to James what was going on with Mako. She stated that the family had to make sure that they got the house in order soon so the cat did not get hurt anymore.

After dinner, Courtney cleared the table and put the dishes in the dish washer. She then went into the living room to join James on the couch. "I took the boys down to the creek today. They had a blast swimming in the water and we had a picnic."

"It sounds like you guys had a fun day," James replied.

"Yeah, we had a good time. I thought I heard a little girl laughing and playing by the water. Must it have been the noises of the creek, I am not used to it," she said to James as she put her feet up on his lap. She wiggled her toes in a way that he knew meant that she wanted her feet rubbed.

"It could have been the noise from the creek or maybe there is a little girl around here. Maybe tomorrow you could take the boys for a walk down the road and see if you can find anyone out here in the country," he said and laughed.

"Maybe I will. Even on this road, there has to be life, right?" she replied with a smile.

"Right," James stated. The two of them watched television for a while and listened to the boys play.

Later that evening, James and Courtney tucked Andy and Billy into bed. They turned off the light in both their rooms and headed to their room. Courtney went into the office and sat at her desk to write while James got into the shower. She could see Mako sitting on the floor in the corner of the room. "I know Mako, this is all new for you, but it will be alright," she said and reached down and pat him on his head and down his back. Then she went back to her desk. She was writing a book about a boy and his friends who found a turtle. They had to figure out how to take turns having the turtle at their houses. In the end, they ended up bringing the turtle to school and making it a classroom pet. She was typing away when James came into the room, "Hey hon, are you almost ready for bed?" he said as he bent down and picked up Mako and held him. He could fell the scratches on his side.

"I am all set here, just saving the file," she replied.

"I see what you meant about the scratches. I think you are right. It was about him getting into things from the move," he said as he put Mako down in the little rocking chair that Courtney kept in the room. "I am sure that he will be alright," he then said as the two of them went off to bed. Courtney and James have been married for over twelve years, and for the first time in a long time, they were both too tired to make love so they just held each other and fell asleep.

James went off to work with lunch in hand and a kiss goodbye leaving Courtney to her work and to tend to the kids. It was about eight am and she was just about to get to work on her book when she noticed Mako digging at the corner of her desk. His paws were covered in blood and he was scratching at the desk with a vengeance. "Mako! She yelled and tried to pick him up. Mako let out a growl and hissed at Courtney. She clapped her hands together and yelled "NO!" Mako snapped out of his trance and tore out of the office and through the bedroom and down the stairs, with Courtney right behind him. "Mako, Mako what the hell is going on with you?" she yelled as she went down the stairs. She found Mako curled up in the corner of the kitchen licking his blood from his paws. She walked up to him and reached her hand out to pet him and Mako tipped his head up to her in acceptance as if nothing had happened upstairs. "I am calling James," she said out loud.

Courtney picked up the phone and called her husband. The phone rang and rang and she got James' voice mail. She did not want him to panic so she simply stated "James hon, I am taking Mako to the vet. I think he may have gotten into something with the move. Love you and see you after work." Then she hung up the phone. She went upstairs and got the boys up and had them get dressed. She explained to them that she wanted to take the cat to the vet. She said it was just for the scratches and got the cat and the kids in the car and headed for the vets office.

Courtney and the boys waited at the vets for a long time before they were seen by the doctor. Once Mako was seen, the doctor ran blood tests, checked his lungs and updated his shots. He also was forced to take x-rays per Courtney's orders. With all tests back, Mako had a clean bill of health. Just as they were leaving the vets office, James called. "Is everything okay with the cat?" James asked.

"He is fine. It was so weird, James,"she said and covered her mouth and the phone receiver and whispered "I found Mako scratching at my desk and his paws were covered in blood and he hissed at me when I tried to pick him up. I thought something was wrong with him, but he is okay according to the vet."

"Well this move has been a lot for him, I guess, but I am glad that he is alright. I will see you tonight when I get home. I love you," James replied.

"Love you too, Bye," Courney stated and hung up.

Courtney and the boys stopped at the grocery store on the way home and picked up a few things for the house. Once home, Courtney put Mako down on the couch and patted his head. He seemed to be doing better, but she wanted to keep an eye on him while she brought in the groceries and started dinner. Andy and Billy went outside to play on the swings and have fun.

With dinner in the oven, Courtney went upstairs to see what could have possibly happened to cause Mako to bleed and act so strange. She walked in her office and saw the pool of blood by the desk. She went into the bathroom to get a rag to clean up the blood off the desk from Mako's paws. "What was he thinking?" she said out loud as she could see the deep claw marks in the wood. "I hope to God that he is going to be okay," she thought. With the blood cleaned up, she tossed the rag in the hamper and went down to play outside with the kids and wait for James to get home from work.

The following morning Courtney sent James off to work, checked on Mako, got the boys and went to the local paint store. She wanted to let the boys pick the colors for their rooms. She laughed so hard when Billy picked lime Green. Andy, on the other hand, picked a light yellow color that pleased Courtney. As they were checking out, Courtney heard "So you bought the old Well's place."

"Excuse me?" Courtney asked.

"The Well's place; that place has been vacant for years, fifty I think. They have remodeled and kept up, but no one has been interested in it. "Sorry, I lost my manners. My name is Jim, Jim Nash. I have lived here in Salem for sixty three years. A beautiful town it is," he said as he shook Courtney's hand.

"Oh, my name is Courtney and this is my youngest Billy and his brother Andy. How did you know we bought the house?"

"Small town; news spreads fast here," he replied.

"Well, it was nice to meet you, Mr.Nash, but we have to go," she said then paid for her paint and left the store.

Billy, Andy, and Courtney spent the rest of day painting. They started with Andy's room. They pulled the furniture away from the wall, laughed and carried on as they taped off the windows and put down the drop cloths and began painting. When they were finished with Andy's room, they moved on to "the green room" as Andy called it. They were half way done when Courtney looked at her watch to see that it was about five pm. She called James and asked him to pick up dinner and then she helped the boys finish Billy's room. Courtney had the boys wash up for dinner while she covered up the paint. Then she washed her hands, went downstairs and set the table for dinner.

James arrived home about six thirty with Chinese food for dinner. He walked in the front door and was met by Courtney. He gave her a big kiss and laughed. "You look beautiful covered in yellow and green paint. Now which one of you boys picked the green?" Billy spoke out loud and proud.

"It was me, Dad, do you like it?"

"I love it," James said with a smile on his face as he reached down with his arms opened and hugged his son."Now let's eat," he stated.

The family sat down at the dining room table eating their dinner talking about Mako and his visit to the vet. With the painting done and the boys cleaned up and sleeping, Courtney explained the real story of Mako and how he was acting."He scared me, James," she said "I have never seen a cat act like that."

"I am sure that you were scared C.J., but a move can upset pets sometimes. They don't know what is going on and it is hard for them to adjust," James stated.

"That's not it, James. I know that's not why he was acting so weird," she replied.

"Okay C.J., you are right. I was not here to see what you saw, so please just calm down. Why don't you go take a shower and

we can try to get some sleep. We will just have to keep an eye on the cat for a few days and see what is going on with him." James said to her as he brushed her hair out of her face.

"Fine, I will take a shower and get ready for bed, but I swear to God, James, if that cat acts out like that again I am going to call you to come home." With that said, James shook his head in agreement and Courtney went off to the shower.

CHAPTER
TWO
THE ARRIVAL

Courtney was finishing the breakfast dishes when she heard
the sound of breaking glass. She dropped the dish rag she was
holding and went into the dining room to find that the boy's picture
from the family picnic had fallen off the wall. Just as she went to
get the broom to clean up the shattered glass, she heard a knock at
the door. She walked to the front door and opened it and there was
a little girl standing there. She was wearing an old fashioned
looking red dress, the kind of dress that you would find at a second
hand store. It had a huge tear in the shoulder and there were stains
all over it like she had been rolling in dirt. Her shoes were black
patent leather and she was wearing an old white sweater that had
three buttons missing. Her hair was a soft blonde color with long
ringlets that were pulled back on both sides with bobby pins. She

had red cheeks and a beautiful smile. "Hello," Courtney said as she knelt down to get a better look at the girl.

"Hi, my name is Linda. I live," then she paused, "I live next door, well, down the road, I was wondering if you had kids that I

could play with?"

"I do, I have two boys. They are upstairs playing in their toy room. "Where did you say you lived?" she said as she got back up.

"I live down the road. My parents are both at work and I just saw you guys move in the other day. I thought you looked nice and there is no one else around here to play with," Linda then said.

"Both your parents are at work? How old are you? You look kind of young to be left alone." Courtney asked.

"I am almost ten. My parents both have to work to pay the bills. I am fine being home alone. The neighbors babysit me. They said I could come over, if it is alright with you," she said with a huge smile on her face.

"As long as your babysitter said you could. I will call the boys down to introduce you," Courtney said.

As it turned out, Linda, Andy, and Billy spent the day playing outside on the swing set with Courtney keeping an eye on them. She was sad to see that Linda was so dirty and wearing such tattered clothes, but she was sure that Linda was happy and that her parents loved her very much. "Must be they are just poor," she said out loud to herself as she watched them swing.

Billy and Andy took turns pushing Linda on the swing and telling her jokes and all about the video games they played. Linda was listening to them with great intent, as if she was hearing about video games for the first time. Billy offered to take her inside to show her how to play the Wii, but she was not ready to leave that swing. "I love to swing! It is so much fun. I feel free when I swing," she said as she giggled. It was after five when Courtney told Linda it was time to go. Courtney needed to get dinner started for her family. "I like the swings; I don't want to go!" Linda yelled.

"I am sorry, Honey. I'm sure your parents will be home soon and looking for you," Courtney said as she stopped the swing.

"Fine, I will go," she said as she got off the swing stomping her feet. "Can I come back tomorrow?" she asked as she looked at Courtney and grabbed her hand.

"I guess, but I need your telephone number so I can make sure it's okay with your Mommy and Daddy," she said.

Linda pulled her hand away, "We, we don't have a phone, but if I could just come over and play, I know it will be okay, please?" she said and took Courtney's hand again.

"Well, I guess, it is still summer vacation and school is starting soon, so I guess you should get all the playing in before you have to go back to school," Courtney said holding her hand and smiling at her.

"Thank you, thank you for letting me come over. I like you; you are a very nice person." With that said, Linda skipped out of the yard and down the road with Courtney watching her until she was out of sight.

James arrived at home about six o'clock as dinner was being put on the table. "Hi Hon, how was your day?" James asked.

"I met a little girl in the neighborhood today, James. I felt so bad for her. Her clothes were all ripped and old, like clothes I had when I was a kid. The boys played with her most of the afternoon on the swings and when it was time for her to go home, she grabbed my hand and almost begged to stay. Also, both her parents work, but they have no phone so I couldn't check to see if she made it home," Courtney replied.

"Well C.J., she probably comes from a family that has a low income and they are just trying to make ends meet. Not everyone has a land phone either. They may only have cell phones," James stated.

"Well, she is coming back over tomorrow and I will ask her about cell phones. "I don't know, James. It's just a feeling I have, but something is not right with her," she said.

"Courtney, you are a worrier. I am sure she just comes from a low income family. Everything will be fine, I am sure," James responded.

"I guess we will wait and see what happens. All I know is that I am going to keep an eye on her," she then said.

James and Courtney sat on the couch watching the news on channel six. They were talking about how the rain was coming in over night when the channel changed to eighteen. Courtney looked at James. "What happened? Are you sitting on the remote?" she asked.

"No, it is right there," he said as he pointed to the coffee table.

Courtney got up and grabbed the remote and put it back on channel six. "Well, that was just weird," she said to James as she cuddled up with him.

"It was weird. Maybe the batteries are low," he replied.

"Could be," Courtney stated.

Later that evening James was fast asleep. Courtney could hear noises coming from Billy's room. Courtney climbed out of her bed. She walked out of her bedroom and into her son's room. Courtney turned on the light to check on her son and saw it, the first real sign that the house was not empty. On the wall written in blood were the words "GET OUT."

"James! James come quickly!" Courtney yelled. James came in the room as Billy sat up in bed rubbing his eyes. By then, the words had disappeared.

"What Courtney? What is it? What's wrong?" James asked.

"I, it was, I don't understand," Courtney stated in a state of confusion. "It was right there, James" she continued. "It was right on that wall. "You saw it right?" she asked as she turned to look at her son.

"No Mom. I only woke up because of the yelling. I didn't see anything, but my bedroom light shining in my eye," Billy replied.

"Saw what, Courtney? You are not making any sense. What did you see?" James asked.

"I saw, well, I saw words on the wall. I swear to God, James," she said looking at her husband. Then she pointed to the wall. "Right there! It said "GET OUT,"written in blood," she continued. "James, I am not crazy. I saw it, plain as I see you standing here. I saw it!" Courtney was beginning to doubt herself. She thought that maybe she was confused. How do words disappear from a wall, and how come her son did not see them?

With all the confusion, James decided to put Billy into Andy's room. He tucked him in next to his brother. Then he took Courtney by the hand and brought her back into Billy's room. "Look Courtney, look at the walls. There is nothing here," he stated. "Just look, there is no sign of writing or blood," he continued. "Please,

please stop this. It must have been a dream that you were having."

"Fine James, I guess you must be right," Courtney replied as they walked out of Billy's room. "I must have dreamt it, and then went into Billy's room." She knew she did not dream it, but what other explanation can there be? It can't just appear and disappear. James turned off the light in Billy's room.

The couple went back in their room and climbed into bed. Courtney layed next to James and put her head on his chest. "James, I am not going crazy, am I?" she asked.

"No, it is just the move and getting settled. You are fine, I promise," James replied.

Courtney closed her eyes. She could not get the image of the words out of her head. "James," she said. "I am going to get in the tub. I need to relax and calm down before I can sleep."

"Okay Courtney, I swear, you are not crazy," James said.

Courtney went into the bathroom, sat down on the edge of the tub, turned on the water and began to cry. "I am not crazy; I saw what I saw," she said and wiped the tears from her eyes. "I know I saw it, no matter what I told James, or what he thinks, I saw it."

Courtney took off her nightgown and got into the tub. She sank down with bubbles all around her. She laid back and closed her eyes. She could feel that James had entered the room. "Hi hon; I will be out in a few minutes. I just need to clear my head," she said. "James? James?" Is that you?" she asked. Then she opened her eyes and saw that the room was empty. "What the hell is going on? I am not crazy!" she said sharply. Courtney got out of the tub, dried off and put her nightgown back on and headed back to her room. She stopped in front of Billy's room, shook her head and proceeded to her room.. She climbed in bed next to James. "Hey, why did you walk out of the bathroom while I was talking to you?" she asked. "James," she whispered. James was fast asleep. "I love you," she said then kissed James on his cheek, rolled over and tried to sleep.

The next day, with James off to work and all the breakfast dishes done, Courtney decided to take the boys to the creek. There were only a few days left before the first day of school began. She packed a lunch, l grabbed her beach blanket and called the kids downstairs. "Get your bathing suits on. We are going to the creek," she stated. The boys ran back up the stairs and got changed. She could hear them talking and laughing. They loved going to the creek since the first day they saw it.

Courtney was sitting on the edge of the water watching the boy's splash and swim. She was trying to write her first poem since the move. She was having a bit of trouble concentrating. She was not sure what the problem was, but something was causing her to have "writers block". Courtney just stared at the paper, hoping that the poem would just tumble out of her head. "Hi Courtney how are you?" Courtney turned to see Linda standing there. She was wearing the same dress, the same shoes and the same sweater.

"Well hello, Linda," she stated. "What are you doing down here without your mother?" she asked.

"My mom is at work; she said I could play with you."

"Do you want to go swimming with the boys?" Courtney asked.

"I, I, I never go near the water," Linda stated. "I have not gone near the water in years."

"Never, what happened, hon, to make you not like the water? Did you fall in or something?" Courtney asked getting up on her knees so she could talk to Linda face to face. "Why don't you like the water?" she asked as she reached out to touch her cheek.

Linda took a few steps back. "I just don't like the water, that's all. I just want to play with you Courtney," she stated.

"Alright," Courtney stated, retracting her hand. "Why don't you sit down and we can talk."

"I don't want to talk. I want to play with you! Didn't you hear me? I want to play," Linda yelled.

"Okay, okay, calm down," Courtney said as she stood up. What do you want to play?"

"You know! You know exactly what I want to play!" Linda screamed.

"Honey, calm down," Courtney said and reached out to touch Linda.

"Don't!" Linda screamed and took off running in the woods.

"Wait, Linda wait!" Courtney wanted to chase after Linda, but she could not leave her boys. All she could do was wait, wait and see if Linda would come back. "What the heck was that all about"? she said.

Courtney stayed down by the water as long as she could. The boys were finished swimming and wanted to go home. She stalled, asking if they wanted to walk by the water, or pick the wild flowers that were growing. The boys, of course, wanted to go home. "Mommy, I want to go home," Andy said.

"Okay boys, let's go," Courtney replied. "Let's go home; I need to get dinner started anyway." She turned and looked into the woods. There was nothing she could do. She needed to take care of her own family. She wanted to help Linda, but Andy and Billy needed her.

Courtney and her family were at the dinner table. She had made a spiral ham and homemade macaroni and cheese. The boys were in the middle of eating their dinner when Courtney stated "I saw Linda today. She was down by the water. She asked me to play. It was weird, James. She got angry with me because I did not know what she wanted to play."

"Well, she is a little girl. Maybe she figured you should know she wanted to play dolls," he said laughing.

"This is not a joke James. She was angry with me, like I should have gotten up and played with her, played the way she wanted,"Courtney replied.

"Courtney, I get it, she was upset with you," he stated.

That evening, Courtney and James tucked the boys into bed, sat down and watched TV. Mako was curled up on Courtney's lap purring away. "I see the cat is feeling more at home" James stated.

"I hope so; he was scaring me the other day," Courtney replied as she continued to stroke his fur. "He still has a few scratches on him, but he looks better" she then said. Courtney could hear someone laughing upstairs. "Boys, go to sleep!" she yelled.

"Courtney, what are you yelling about? The boys are asleep." James stated.

"I can hear one of them laughing James," she replied.

"I will go check. I am telling you that they are both asleep," James said as he headed to the stairs. Courtney decided to go with her husband, so she got off the couch and grabbed her husband's hand. Together, they walked up the stairs and checked both bedrooms. James was correct. Both of the boys were sleeping."I don't understand. I could hear laughter. I could hear it James, hear it coming from up here," Courtney said looking confused. James put his arm around his wife and escorted her to the bedroom.

"It has been a long few weeks; the move, the unpacking, getting the boys settled in. It is a lot to take in," he said.

"Maybe that is what it is, but what if it is something else?" she asked. "What if this house really does want us out?" she asked.

"C.J., a house can't want you out. I really truly think that you are just overwhelmed. The boys will be going back to school in a few days and then you will be able to get back to your writing. That will help settle your mind and you will feel better." James leaned over and kissed his wife on her cheek. "Trust me, you will be fine," he continued. "Just relax; it is just the changing of houses. It is making you imagine things."

"Whatever you think James," she said. The whole time she was thinking to herself "It is this house, the house wants something from me, and I will figure this out"

This night, the family was tucked in their beds fast asleep. There were no words on the walls, no unexplained laughter. There was just silence. Courtney laid there in her bed waiting, just waiting for something to happen in the night that would help James understand. She laid there almost daring the house to say something. Silence was the answer she got.

CHAPTER

THREE

BACK TO SCHOOL

Courtney had walked the boys to the end of the road to the bus stop. She locked the camera on her boys and took tons of pictures. Billy and Andy were dressed in their brand new shoes, crisp new shirts and jeans. She was so excited to see her boys starting a new school. She just wanted to capture all the memories that they had to offer. Andy as usual, was being a big ham, posing for his mother, making funny faces in the camera. "Hi Courtney," this little voice said. Courtney turned around to see Linda standing there.

"Well hello, Linda, she said, noticing that Linda was wearing the same old dress she wore every time she saw her. "Are you excited about going back to school?" Courtney asked.

"I, well, I, I don't go to school," Linda stated.

"What? Are you home schooled?" Courtney asked as the bus drove up and she waved goodbye to her boys.

I don't want to talk about that; I want to play" Linda replied.

"I know, but little girls need to learn," Courtney said as she knelt down to Linda's level.

"I said! I want to play! Why won't you play with me like they did?" Linda yelled.

"Alright, calm down who are "They" and what do I have to play?" Courtney asked.

"You know! You have to know! Now let's play!" Linda yelled.

"I assure you, Linda," Courtney said. "I don't know what you are talking about. I don't know who "they" are or what "they" played. I would love to play with you, but I need you to tell me what we are playing," Courtney replied still confused about Linda's request.

"Never mind I will have to show you another time! I have to go!" Linda yelled and ran down the road. Courtney chased

after her.

"Wait! Linda wait I want to play!" Courtney screamed. As she rounded the corner, she noticed that Linda was gone. "Where did she go?" Courtney asked out loud.

Courtney walked back to the house, went inside and walked directly to her office. She sat at her computer and turned it on. She took the memory stick out of her camera and put it into the slot in the front of the computer. She got all the pictures she wanted and printed them out and framed them. She then hung the pictures in the dining room, all the while she was thinking about Linda. "How could her parents not put her in school?" she thought.

When Courtney was finished hanging her pictures, she got started with her house cleaning. She had the laundry in the washer and the dishes done. She was so used to playing with the boys, that she did not know what to do. She decided to go up and try to write a new book. She was at her desk, but she could not concentrate. All she could think about was Linda. She could not understand why she was not in school. Why would her parents not home school her at the very least? She wanted to meet her parents to get to the truth, to find out what was going on with this girl. Why did she wear the same clothes every day and why did she get so upset about not knowing how to play her game. "She just seems so angry, I don't understand I am lost," she thought. "I can't concentrate right now," she said out loud.

Courtney got up from her desk, went to the window and looked outside. It was a beautiful September day. The leaves were just beginning to change on the trees and the wind was blowing a late summer breeze into the bedroom. Courtney took a deep breath. "That's it, I will go for a walk and see if I can find where this girl lives," she stated. Courtney went downstairs and got on her sneakers. She grabbed the spare house key by the front door and walked outside. She walked down the dirt road. She could hear the creek running down behind the houses as she walked. The neighbor's dog began to bark. She was happy it was tied up. Then she continued to walk to the dead end sign. "Well, I can't figure out what house is hers. There are only eight houses on this street, but not one has any signs of children playing," she said out loud and turned and headed for home.

Back at the house, Courtney went to the kitchen, got a glass of water and drank it. She then turned and headed to the living room.

She sat on the couch, turned on the television and watched the news for a bit. The whole while, she was thinking about Linda. This beautiful little girl who seemed so lost in this world. This was a little girl whose own family did not send her to school or dress her properly. She wanted so badly to reach out to this family and help them, if she could only find them.

Later that afternoon, Courtney was home with her boys from the bus stop. They had both told her about their first day of school and their new teachers and friends. She had dinner going on the stove and she was just waiting for James to come home. She could hear the boys laughing and playing in the toy room. She was smiling as she set the table for dinner, happy that the boys were home from school. She had missed the sound of children playing.

As she finished setting the table, the phone rang. Courtney headed out to the kitchen and answered the phone. "Hello,"

she said.

"Hi Honey, just checking in to see how you are doing," her mom said.

"Hi Mom, I am fine, just getting back to normal life now that the boys are in school," Courtney replied.

"Well, that is another reason why I called, I wanted to check on the boys first day at their new school,'' she stated.

"Well, Billy got off the bus and talked my ear off about his new teacher and how he made a ton of friends today. He went on and on the whole way home. Andy was not even able to tell me about his day until we got home. Once he had a chance, he said it went well, but I think that he needs more time to get used to a new school," Courtney said.

"Well, it sounds like things are going to be alright then. Glad to hear that Billy is so excited, and don't worry, Andy will be fine. He is just used to his school and his friend's hon, but he will adjust just fine. Do you remember when we moved when you were about seven?" she asked.

"No, not really," Courtney replied.

"Well your Dad and I bought the house we still live in when you were about seven years old and you had to start a new school. I remember you were scared to start, but within a week, you had friends," she continues. "Your grades were better in the new school than they were in the old school. Sometimes, a change can be a good thing," Courtney's mom said.

"Thanks Mom, I feel better. I think sometimes I just need to hear your opinion, and I feel better," Courtney said.

"Your welcome, tell the boys I said hello, I have to run to the store for Dad so I have to go," she replied.

"Okay, I will tell them. Tell Dad I love him," Courtney replied.

"I will, bye," she said.

Courtney hung up the phone, went to the stairs and yelled, "Boys, Grammy called. She just wanted to say she loves you and she is glad you had a good first day!"

"Alright Mom!" the boys yelled almost at the same time. Then Courtney went back to the kitchen and continued to prepare dinner.

James came home at about six thirty pm. He walked in the front door and was greeted by both of his boys. "Dad," Billy said as he hugged his father. "Today was the best day ever!" he began. "I love my teacher, and the new school is awesome!" he continued. "I have a seat in the front row next to her desk, and she made me feel welcome in the class." As, Billy continued to talk, Andy hugged his father and went to the dining room table and sat down as his mom put dinner on the table. When Billy was finished filling his father in about his day, he went to the table as well.

"So," James said as he sat down at the table. "How was your day, Andy?"

"Well, I guess it was good. I just miss my old friends," he replied.

"I know sometimes it is hard to start a new school," James said. "I am sure that in time, you will make friends and you will be fine; just give it a few days. You are a smart, funny boy and everyone will want to be your friend," James continued. "You have lots of friends back in the city, so I am sure you will have lots here too."

"Thanks Dad," Andy replied. "I feel better."

Courtney kissed Andy on the forehead, served him his dinner and sat down at the table next to him. "I know that tomorrow will be a better day, and then by next week, you will forget you even missed your old school and friends," Courtney said.

Then the family enjoyed their dinner as James talked about his day at work, and all about the new project that he was in charge of.

Later on that evening, Courtney was in the office writing her book. A book that she had titled "BACK TO SCHOOL THE NEW BEGINNING." She could hear the boys in the other room playing, and James was on their bed watching the evening news. "Courtney, come check this out," James said. Courtney got up from her desk and entered the bedroom.

"What's up?" she asked.

"Check out the weather for this evening," he said. Courtney turned her attention to the television.

"The cold front will be colliding with the warm front coming down from the north. This will cause a very large electrical storm in most of the viewing area. There may be power outages due to high winds. This storm may be bringing hail as well," the news reporter said. "This is the number you should call if you lose power or see fallen power lines" she continued as the television flashed a number across the screen. "We are asking all viewers to take caution if they are on the roads and those who are inside, to stay inside. The storm is due to hit around ten pm. this evening," she reported.

"Wow, James, this could be a big storm," Courtney stated as she sat down on the bed next to him.

"I think so. I am going to put your car and the truck in the garage C.J., I will be right back," James said as he got up from the bed and grabbed his slippers.

"Alright, I am going to go tell Billy to get in the shower and get ready for bed. Then I am going to get back to my work," she said following him to the door.

Courtney entered the toy room and began to laugh. Andy and Billy had built a whole town with Lincoln logs and the cat was standing in the middle of it. He looked like Godzilla in the center of Tokyo! She could not help herself. She had to say it. "Well hello, Catzilla," she laughed as she bent over and pet her cat.

"Catzilla?" Andy questioned.

"Yes Catzilla, like Godzilla, only cuter," Courtney replied.

"Mom, you're funny," Billy said.

"I know. Billy I need you to get in the shower and get cleaned up for bed. Tomorrow is another school day."

"Fine Mom," he replied and got up and went into his room and grabbed clean boxers and a shirt.

"As for you Andy, as soon as he is out, it is your turn. Until then, keep an eye on Catzilla; he may wreck your village," she said smiling down at Mako who let out a meow.

"I will Mommy," Andy stated as Courtney was walking out the door.

With the boys both washed up and tucked into bed, and James lying in bed watching television, Courtney decided to get back to work. She walked into her office and sat down in her computer chair. She put her glasses on and got back to work. The minute she sat down, Mako jumped up on her lap and curled up. "Well Mr. Mako, how can I get anything done with you on my lap?" she said as she smiled. Then she turned her attention back to her work.

Courtney had been working for about an hour when the storm came in. She was in the middle of typing a sentence when the thunder began to roll and the storm raged outside the window. At this point, Mako had already left her lap and she was the only one awake in the house. She finished her sentences and decided to save her work in case the power went out. She clicked on "SAVE FILE," then finished shutting down the computer. She got up from her desk and headed toward bed. She stopped in front of the window to check out the storm. She could see something moving by the swing set, but she could not make it out. She walked back over to her desk and grabbed her glasses and walked back over to the window. She cupped her hands to the sides of her face, and looked out the glass. At this point, there was someone, not something, by the swing set. "What the hell? Who would be out on a night like this, and in my yard?" She squinted her eyes a bit, and then looked again. "That's Linda!" she yelled waking James with her words.

Courtney raced down the stairs, grabbed her shoes and stumbled as she tried to put them on. She hurried over to the closet next to the bathroom, grabbed her rain coat, and put it over her shoulders as she rushed to the front door. She threw her hood up over her hair and walked off the front porch. "Who's there?" she yelled as she walked toward the swing set. The rain was pouring down on Courtney. She was soaked. She was having a hard time seeing, but she was not giving up. She continued to walk across the drive way. She could see, that now, the person was on the swing. "Who's there?" she yelled again, as the rain was pounding down on her face, almost choking her as she talked.

"Courtney!" James yelled as he grabbed her by the arm. "What the hell are you doing out here?" he continued.

"There is someone out here, James, I saw something on the swing!" she screamed over the storm.

"Courtney, there is no one out here! Please come in the house!" James replied as he was getting soaked by the storm.

"I saw someone James, and I think it was a child!" she yelled, trying to pull away from James.

"Okay, let's go check it out, but I am telling you, I was watching from the window and you are the only person out here in the rain."

James and Courtney walked over to the swing set. They were both dripping wet and Courtney's glasses were all fogged up. At this point, she had to rely on James to lead her. "See Courtney, there is nothing here," James said. "There is no one on the swing set," he continued, with the rain pounding down on him. "Please,

please Courtney, let's just go inside."

"James, I saw someone here! I am not crazy; I saw someone!" she yelled as James took her by the arm and gently walked her toward the house.

"Okay, C.J., whatever you say, just please come in the house and we can talk about it there," James said, continuing to help his wife back to the house.

Courtney entered the house with James right behind her. He helped her take off her coat.

"Stay right here honey and I will get you a towel." James took off his wet shirt and walked to the bathroom and threw it in the washer. He then grabbed a towel off the rack for Courtney who was standing just inside the front door with her glasses in her hand and tears streaming down her face.

James took the towel and wrapped it around Courtney's shoulders. "Let's get you upstairs and into a hot bath before you get sick. Come on, hon, you are shivering," James said helping her to the stairs.

"James," Courtney said, "I don't understand what is happening to me. I am not crazy. I saw something," she continued as they walked up the stairs.

"I know C.J., I know," James said as he helped his wife into the bathroom. "Why don't you just sit down and I will get the water going for you," James said, realizing that he was dripping wet and freezing himself.

"Thank you," Courtney replied with tears flowing so hard that she could not even see anything anymore.

Courtney's husband carefully took her by the hand, and helped her take the towel off her shoulders. He then gently helped get her night shirt off and her panties. He took her by the hand and led her to the tub. "Here, hon, let me help you get it," he stated. Then helped Courtney get herself settled into the water. "Are you going to be alright in here if I go change my clothes?" he asked.

"I will be fine," she answered. "James, before you go, do you really believe I am losing my mind?" she asked as she wiped the final tear from her eye.

"No, you're not losing your mind; the rain can play tricks on you. You are fine; now you just relax in the tub. I will be back after I change my clothes and clean up the water. I love you C.J." he said. Then he bent down, kissed his wife on her forehead, grabbed a towel, and walked out of the bathroom.

James went into the bedroom, turned on the light and went to his dresser. He was shivering cold at this point and needed to get dry clothes on. James got out clean boxers, pajama pants and a tee shirt and put them on. He grabbed all the wet things and carried them down to the washer. When that was finished, he grabbed another towel and began to clean up the water in front of the door and added that towel to the wash as well. He then went back up to be with his wife. James opened the bathroom door to find Courtney in her bathrobe sitting on the floor. "Courtney, are you alright?" he asked.

"I'm fine, just sitting here. I guess I didn't feel like a bath. I did clean up the water for you," she said.

"I see that. Thanks, but really, why are you sitting on the floor?" he asked as he offered her a hand to get up.

"I got down here to clean up the water. Then I thought about the rain storm and the fact that I thought I saw someone out there and I just stayed on the floor," she replied taking James' hand and getting to her feet.

"It's going to be fine C.J. Let's just get you back to bed. You just need to rest," James said.

"James, you might be right," she stated as the couple walked into the bedroom. Courtney could see out the window that the storm was still raging. "James, I have to look, just to make sure that no one is there," Courtney stated.

"I will look with you," he said and walked to the window with his wife. "See Courtney," he said. "There is nothing out this window but rain."

"James, I really think I need help. I have seen blood on the walls, I heard voices down by the water, and now this," she said as she began to cry.

"You just need to get some rest. You will see that everything will be fine," he stated and kissed his wife on her cheek. He then put his arm around her back and gently encouraged her to walk away from the window.

James pulled the covers back on the bed on his wife's side, helped her in and covered her up. He then went and turned the bedroom light off and climbed in on his side. Courtney rolled over and put her head on her husband's chest. "Are you sure that I am not crazy?" she asked.

"Yes honey, I am sure. Just try to rest," he said as he ran his fingers down her cheek and brushed her hair off her face.

CHAPTER

FOUR

THE DOCTOR'S OFFICE

Courtney kissed James goodbye, put her boys on the bus and now was home alone. She knew that James believed she was fine, but she had concerns of her own that she was not. She got out the phone book and looked for a physician in the area. She wanted to have some testing done, testing to see if she had something wrong with her brain, her vision, something. She needed something to explain what she was seeing and what was happening to her. She needed to start with a general check up. She came across a doctor's office that accepted James insurance and called the office. She explained that she was new in town and she was looking to have a checkup completed. The receptionist stated that they could see her today to get the necessary paper work done and to at least meet the doctor. The appointment was set for eleven thirty. "Great, thank you, I will see you at eleven thirty," she said and hung up the phone and got into the shower.

With the shower running, and Courtney just about ready to get it into it, she heard the door open down stairs. "I know I locked that door," she said out loud. Courtney quickly grabbed a towel to cover up, opened the bath room door and went to the top of the stairs. "Hello," she called out. "Hello is anyone there?" she asked. Courtney slowly walked down the stairs and peaked around the corner into the living room. There was no one to be seen, so she continued into the living space. "Hello?" she called out again as she looked over at the front door. She could see that the door was still locked. "What the hell is happening to me?" she said out loud. "I am going crazy," she said and headed back up the stairs and got into the shower.

When Courtney was finished showering, she got dressed and grabbed her keys. She went out to the garage and climbed into her blue Subaru Outback and closed the door. She pushed the button to open the garage, and backed out. Courtney drove into town looking for Oak Street. She was not sure where it was, so she looked at the directions that the receptionist had given her. When she found the office, she parked the car, took a deep breath and grabbed her wallet and got out of the car. She pushed the lock on her keys and headed to the door.

Courtney entered Doctor Lancaster's office. She walked up to the receptionist counter. "Hi, my name is Courtney Stealth. I called earlier about getting a new doctor. I have an appointment."

"Yes, I see it right here. I have some paperwork for you. I also need a copy of your insurance card," the lady said as she stood up and leaned over the counter. "You need to make sure you sign here, initial this page as well,"she said as she turned the page.

"Thank you," Courtney stated and took a seat and began to fill out the papers. When she was finished, she gave the paperwork and her insurance card to the receptionist then waited for her to make a copy. Then took her insurance card and sat back down, put it away, and waited for her name to be called.

Courtney sat for about ten minutes before the nurse called her name. She got up and followed her to a little room on the left side of the hallway. She entered the room, sat down and the nurse began to talk to her. "I see here that this is your first visit," she began.

"Yes" Courtney replied. "We just moved up here from the city and I figured I should get a doctor in the area."

"Well, it looks like all the papers are filled out. The doctor will be with you in a few minutes," she stated as she walked out, closing the door behind her. "What am I going to tell the doctor about why I am here? I am perfectly healthy, just seeing things that are not really there. Can't really tell him that now, can I?" She thought to herself.

Doctor Lancaster knocked on the door, opened it and walked in. "Hi, I am Doctor Lancaster," he stated, holding his hand out to shake Courtney's.

"I 'm Courtney Stealth. It is nice to meet you," she replied.

"So," he said as he sat down in the chair next to her. "What seems to bring you to see me today?"

"Well, I just moved up here from the city and I wanted to get a doctor in the area" she replied.

"I am sure there is a reason you need a doctor, or you would not be here. So what is it? Not sleeping well with the move? Allergies acting up now that you are in the country? There has to be something. Or is this just a routine checkup?" he said with a smile on his face.

"Well," Courtney had to think fast. "I have been getting headaches, and sometimes it affects my sleep," she stated.

"Now we are getting somewhere," he replied. "Headaches can be caused by lots of things including stress, change of jobs, family problems. That kind of thing happening?" he asked.

"No, the family is wonderful. Kids are great and my husband James is wonderful. I am a writer of children's books, so there is no stress in doing that," she replied.

"Well, it could be other things too. What do you think is causing it, Courtney?" he asked.

"Well," she began, I really don't know," she stated. Thinking the whole time, I am going crazy; that's what I think it is! I am a nut job! ""I have not changed anything. My diet is the same, my routine is the same. So I guess I was hoping you could help me figure it out," she stated, looking at the doctor for answers as to why she is crazy.

"If there is no real change in your life, and you are eating well, the only thing I can say is to keep an eye on it and see when the headaches are coming and we can try to narrow it down," the doctor stated.

"Doctor Lancaster, I really feel that something is wrong with me. Could it be a tumor?" she asked.

"At your age and the fact that you are still able to do daily living without too much trouble, I really doubt that it is a tumor," the doctor said.

"You don't understand, I need an answer to what is going on with me," she demanded.

"Look Mrs. Stealth, I don't know what you expect me to do." he questioned.

Courtney had to think for a moment. She took a deep breath and said "Alright, here is the truth. I am seeing things and I can't figure out why."

"What kind of things are you seeing?" the doctor asked.

"Sometimes it is images outside the window and other times I am seeing things written on the wall that no one else can see," she replied.

"Alright, maybe we need to do further testing. I suggest a CAT scan, just to rule out a problem in the brain. I am sure it will come back fine, but it may help you feel better to have it done," he said.

"What do you think?" he then asked.

"I think you are correct. It will make me feel better," she replied, thinking to herself "I hope it shows something to explain what I have been seeing, and hearing.

Doctor Lancaster wrote up the prescription for Courtney to have the CAT scan, shook her hand and told her that when she has completed the CAT scan to schedule an appointment to see him again and they would go over the results together. He also gave her a prescription for pain medication for the headaches she claimed she had. With both prescriptions in hand, she headed back to the receptionist.

"All set?" she asked as she reached for the paperwork from the doctor.

"I need to schedule a CAT scan," Courtney stated.

"I see that. Let me call that department and see when we can get that done," the receptionist stated.

"It looks like they can get you in tomorrow at ten thirty am., is that a good time for you?" she asked.

"Tomorrow will be fine. Then I need to come back here to get the results," she continued.

"I can get you in tomorrow at one pm. That should give the doctor enough time to call over and get the results," the receptionist said.

"That will be fine. I will see you tomorrow," she stated and walked out the door.

Courtney got in her car, started it up and headed for Wal Mart. She needed to get a few things for home, and wanted to grab something for dinner because she neglected to take something out of the freezer. She parked her car and went inside. She grabbed a cart and went to the freezer section. She knew the kids would be perfectly happy with frozen pizza, so she grabbed a few of them and then got French bread pizza for her and James. She then went and got cat food for Mako, some laundry soap, and headed for the checkout line.

Courtney checked out, got in her car and headed for home. She passed the library on the way home, thinking to herself "Maybe I can take the boys there sometime. They probably have a great children's section which the boys would love. And check to see if they stock any of my books," she smiled at the thought of her books making their way to this small town. "It would be interesting if people knew I was a published author. I may even become a local celebrity," she said out loud and laughed. "That would be too funny. The boys would have all their friends getting my autograph," she said, laughing at herself.

Courtney pulled up to the mail box at the end of the road just before the boys got off the bus. She grabbed the mail and decided to wait for them instead of going home. She waited only a few minutes and the bus arrived. Both boys got into the car. "Mom, I had a great day. You were right; I made friends today, Jake and Tyler. They want me to join the soccer team. Can I, Mom, can I join? Practice is on Tuesday's and Thursday's and the games are on Saturday mornings. Please Mom, please can I join?" Andy asked.

"Let me talk to Dad, but I am sure that it will be okay," she replied.

"How was your day, Billy?" she asked. "My day was good, Mom. I really like my new school."

Courtney brought in the groceries and the boys took off for the swing set. It was still warm in early September, so they came running in to ask if they could go to the creek or swim in the pool. Courtney agreed to let them swim in the pool before she started the pizza. She grabbed her laptop out of the office and headed outside to watch her boys. She sat down in the lounge chair and watched as her boys took turns doing cannon balls off the diving board. She was trying to work on her new book, but it was impossible to do with the boys having so much fun. "Hey, you want some company?"she asked.

"Mom, you're coming in?" Billy asked.

"I was thinking about it," Courtney replied.

"Come on, Mom; go get your suit on. We want you to come in!" Andy said Excitedly.

"Get out for a second while I go change, then we can all swim together," she said.

"Alright," the boys replied and got out of the pool.

Courtney hurried up into the house, grabbed her bathing suit off the back of the downstairs bathroom door and put it on. She grabbed a beach towel out of the bathroom closet and headed out to the pool. She laid the towel down on the lounge chair and dove into the pool. Andy and Billy jumped in after her. The boys spent the next hour splashing around the pool with their mother. She was laughing and playing with her boys, forgetting about the night before and the doctor visit today. Courtney was having fun, fun just being a mom and not thinking about Linda or what happened to Mako or the writing on the wall or the storm last night; she was just having fun.

Courtney and the boys got out of the pool just before five pm. She needed to get the pizza cooking so dinner would be ready when James came home. She came inside and toweled off and changed her clothes. She sent her boys upstairs to change as well, with a reminder that they needed to hang their bathing suits out on the railing after they changed. She went into the living room and set up TV trays. She thought that the boys would love to watch television while they ate dinner. She was just about to take the pizza out of the oven when James came in the front door. "Hi, hon," Courtney called. "I am getting the pizza out of the oven. I will be right there," she continues to say as she put the pizza pans on the counter. She was just headed out to greet James when he entered the kitchen. He kissed his wife and said,

"How was your day? Do you feel better than last night?"

"My day went fine. I just worked on my book," she lied. "I feel much better today. I am so sorry about last night."

"Let it go, Courtney. I am just glad that you are alright. Let's eat," he continued."French bread pizza, yum. We haven't had that in a long time. Let me help you set the boy's plates," he said.

James went to the stairs and called the boys down for dinner. They came running, stopping to hug their father along the way. Andy grabbed the remote and turned the channel to cartoons, to see that Sponge Bob was on. "Can we watch this, Mom?"

"It's fine with me ask Dad."

"I don't care," James said to his son as he sat down in the recliner.

The family ate their dinner while they talked about the day they had. Courtney, told James about Andy wanting to join soccer. His response was "yes". When dinner was finished, the boys went to the kitchen table to work on homework while Courtney cleaned up. James was relaxing in his chair watching the news, falling asleep almost immediately. James always claims he is "resting his eyes" and "listening" to the television. He could never admit that he falls asleep frequently.

With the kitchen cleaned and homework done, the kids left the kitchen and headed outside to play. They were riding their bikes in the driveway. Billy was making engine sounds as he raced his bike down the driveway to the ramp that Andy had built. The two of them were laughing and challenging each other to jump higher than the last jump. Courtney was sitting on the porch with a glass of iced tea, smiling at her boys having fun. She was just about to take a sip of tea when the phone rang.

Courtney grabbed the cordless phone off the table, and answered it. "Hello?" she asked.

"Hi C.J., it's Brenda. Is James right there?" She asked.

"Hi, he is but he is sleeping. Do you want me to wake him up?" Courtney asked.

"No, I was just calling to see how everyone was doing," she said. "Are the boys doing well in their new school?" she asked.

"Oh yeah, Billy and Andy both like it. Andy is going to join the soccer team," Courtney stated.

"Really," Brenda stated. "That's great. Can I talk to the boys?" she asked.

"Sure, hold on. I will get Billy first," Courtney stated. "Billy, get off your bike and come to the phone. It's Grandma Brenda" she said.

"Okay" Billy replied.

Billy and Andy took turns talking to their grandmother about the new school and how they were making new friends. Billy talked for about ten minutes. He could not get all the information out. He was talking so fast that Courtney had to remind him to slow down so Grandma Brenda could understand him. Andy told her he could not believe it had only been two days, and how he wanted to get on the soccer team with Jake and Tyler.

When the boys were finished talking, Courtney took the phone back. "I think James is up. I will go check." Courtney walked into the house and sure enough, James was awake watching the news. "James, it's your mom," she stated and handed the phone to her husband.

"Hi Mom," James said.

"Hi, I was checking in to see how you guys were all doing. It's so different having to call you up there. I miss being able to just drive five minutes down the road to see you," she said.

"I know Mom. We will have to have you stay with us some weekend," James said.

"Any weekend you want to. You just let us know and we will make up the spare bed in the office," James continued.

"Well, let's see how the boys do for the first few weeks of school and maybe I could come up for Billy's birthday," she replied.

"That sounds like a good idea, Mom. I am not sure what kind of party we are going to have yet. It depends on the weather, but you are coming up that weekend even if I have to come and get you. You know that we miss you," he stated.

"I know," she replied.

Later that evening, James and Courtney had tucked the boys into bed, and they were on the couch watching a movie. They talked about his mom coming to town and what they were going to do about Billy's party. They figured if the weather was still nice, they could have a pool party. If not, they would set it up in the garage. Courtney told James that she would have to get the invitations out soon, because if some of his friends from the city want to come, they would need to have some notice. They also decided that they would let Billy invite friends from school as well. "I hope he doesn't get upset if all his friends from the city don't come. It would be a very long drive for their parents," Courtney stated.

"He will understand, maybe we could go to the city and have a separate party at my mom's house for his friends down there," James stated.

"James, that is a great idea." Call your mom tomorrow and ask her. That way Billy will get to see a lot of his old friends and so will we," Courtney said excitedly.

"I will call her on my lunch break," James replied getting up from the couch. "I'm tired C.J. I am going to bed. Are you coming up?" he asked.

"Yeah" she said, getting up from the couch. "I am not tired, but I should work on my book," she continued. "I really think this is going to be a good one, James," she said as they walked up the stairs.

Courtney worked on her book for a few hours, typing away at her computer with her husband snoring in the other room. She could tell she was getting tired. Her eyes felt heavy and her contacts were getting dry. She got up from the computer and went into the bathroom. She took out her contacts, grabbed her glasses and headed back to her desk. She saved the chapter she was working on, clicked on shut down, turned the computer off and headed to bed.

The next morning, Courtney made James' lunch and he was off to work. She gave the boys breakfast and walked them down to the end of the street to wait for the bus. She looked around, half expecting to see Linda walking down the street. She realized that she did not see her yesterday. She hoped that she was alright. She then headed back to the house to get in the shower. She needed to make sure she was ready to go to her doctor's appointment on time.

Courtney was dressed and ready to go. She was feeling bad because James had no clue what she was doing. For the first time ever, Courtney kept the truth from her husband. She was just scared that if he knew, he would worry that something was really wrong with his wife. She had to try to let that go, and get to the CAT scan. She arrived at the appointment about five minutes early, just long enough to get the paper work done. She was called into the room where the CAT scan machine was. It was a small room, too small, Courtney thought, too small for such a large machine. The technician checked to make sure that Courtney had taken off all her jewelry, and reminded her that the machine would be loud, and at times, she would have to hold very still. When the scan was done, Courtney climbed off the table. She was happy that she was able to leave that tiny room. She was normally not claustrophobic, but this tiny room, being put inside this machine, could make anyone fearful. She then picked up her wedding ring and her watch off the stand and put them back on, and grabbed her purse and headed out to her car.

With about a half hour remaining before the doctor's appointment, Courtney decided to get a bite to eat. She walked into Wendy's, ordered a salad, fries, and sat down and ate her lunch, thinking about the CAT scan the whole time. "Please God, make sure that everything is okay," she thought to herself. "If everything is okay, then I must be crazy for seeing what I have seen and hearing what I have heard. I don't know what I want the results to be," she continued to think. Courtney shook her head, finished her lunch, and tossed out her garbage. She took her keys out of her purse and headed to her car. She got inside, put the key in the ignition, and backed out of her parking spot and headed to the doctor's office.

Courtney arrived at Doctor Lancaster's office just after one o'clock. She walked into the waiting room, checked in with the receptionist, sat down and waited for the nurse to call her name. She could see that there were a few others waiting as well. She hoped that she would be called in first. She really needed to get the results and get home. She was beginning to have second thoughts about not telling James. She took her cell phone out of her purse, fiddled with it in her hand. "Should I call him?" she thought, and then shook her head. "No, I am doing this on my own. If I tell him now, he will be upset that I held the truth from him." She put the phone back in her purse.

"Courtney," the nurse called.

Courtney got up from her chair feeling a bit shaky. She was nervous about what she was going to hear. She followed the nurse into the first room on the right. There was no exam table in this room, just a few chairs and the doctor's desk. She wondered if this was a sign of bad news ready to happen. "The doctor will be right with you," the nurse stated as she closed the door behind her on the way out. "Well, there is no turning back now. Please find some explanation, something that is causing what I see and hear. Hell, I don't want to have anything wrong with me," she thought. Her mind was racing, racing with thoughts of what she has been seeing and what test she had just completed. She was about to grab her phone again, thinking she wanted her husband, when the doctor came in. "Hello again Mrs. Stealth," the doctor stated as he entered the room. "I have the results of your test," he said as he sat down behind his desk. "Let's see what the results say," he stated as he looked over the fax that he received.

"Okay," Courtney said as she crossed her legs and leaned forward toward his desk.

"Everything looks fine here," he stated. Courtney took a deep breath and leaned back into her chair.

"So, what do we do about your headaches? We could run more tests," the doctor said.

"No, I think maybe it is just from the move. Maybe I over reacted," she said. The only test Courtney wanted was the one that says she is not crazy. "Do they have a test for that," she thought to herself.

"Well, if you want more testing done, just let me know," he

stated as he got up and shook her hand. "It is nice to have you as a new patient," he continued as Courtney got up to shake his hand.

"Thank you Doctor Lancaster, and if the headaches don't go away soon, I will come back for more testing," she stated as the two of them left the office.

All the way home, Courtney was deep in thought about her test results and about Linda. Her mind was racing with thoughts. She was having a hard time focusing on the road ahead of her. When she arrived at the mail box, she decided to drive home, and then walk to the bus stop to get the boys. This way she could get dinner started before they came home.

Back at the house, Courtney went to the refrigerator. She got out the pork chops she had set aside for tonight's dinner. She took the pork chops out of the package and covered them with seasoning. She looked at the clock and realized that it was time to get the boys. She went to the door and walked down to the bus stop.

Andy and Billy got off the bus, both of them smiling. They were excited to be home. It was Friday and they were looking forward to the weekend. Since they moved, their dad had been telling them that he was going to take them camping, and this was the weekend that he was going to do it.

The boys were packing up all the gear that they needed and putting it on the porch, while Courtney finished getting dinner in the oven. When she had finished, she went upstairs and packed the boys clothes and other necessities in their backpacks. She then gathered up James' things and tossed them into his father's old Army bag. It was ugly and green, but James loved it.

When Courtney was finished, she tossed the sleeping bags down the stairs, gathered up the backpacks and James' bag and carried them down to the living room. She could see that the boys had found the Coleman lantern, the cooler, tents, and the portable grill and put them on the porch.

They were working hard to get the things ready before their father came home. Courtney called to the boys through the open window to come get their bags. She then went to the kitchen to start the vegetables for dinner. Billy came running in. "Mom, where is the water cooler?" he asked. "Andy and I can't find it in the garage."

"I will go look for it in a minute. Just let me get the veggies in the microwave. Did you get everything else done Hon?" she asked.

"We have everything I think, Mom, but could you just check and make sure?" he asked.

"Sure can," she said as she closed the microwave door and started the vegetables.

Courtney went out to the garage with both boys right behind her. She looked around and could not find the cooler. She moved the tarp that was used to cover up the pool and there it was. She needed to clean it up, so she brought it over to the hose.

"Andy, do me a favor and go get me the dish detergent," she stated to her son as she started to rinse out the water cooler. When Andy returned with the soap, Courtney finished washing out the cooler and filled it with fresh cold water and carried it to the porch. She then went back into the house and set the table for dinner. She could hear James' truck pull into the driveway. They were so excited that they didn't even let him out of the truck before they started talking to him. She could also hear the boys telling their father about all the things they had ready for their trip as they walked to the house.

The family sat at the dinner table and talked about the camping trip. The boys were asking their mom what she packed for them in their backpacks. She explained that she packed bathing suits, pajamas, shorts, tee shirts and other essentials needed for camping. James laughed at the fact that he didn't have to pack anything, just load it into the truck. "Sure, James, must be nice to just come home and have it done," Courtney teased.

"It is," he said laughing, as he got up from the table. "I am going to get in the shower and change, and then I will load up the truck," James stated as he headed for the stairs. "I want you boys to get showered before we leave," he continued. "It is going to be a few days without a shower and I want you cleaned up before we go. By the way, Mom said yes to the party," James stated as he walked up the stairs.

Courtney got the cooler off the porch. She filled it with eggs, milk, bacon, hot dogs, hamburger, and all the other things that they would need for the weekend. She grabbed the Styrofoam cups out of the cupboard and the paper plates, and finished getting the rest of the items they would need. When she was finished, she took the bags out to the truck and put them in the back seat. She was headed back to the porch when James came out of the house. He helped Courtney finish loading the rest of the stuff into the truck.

Courtney carried Billy out to the truck. "I am going to miss you so much," she said as she kissed her son and buckled him in the truck. She then turned her attention to Andy, who was waiting for his kiss goodbye. He climbed into the truck and sat down and buckled up next to his brother. She reached over, hugged her son and kissed him on his forehead. "I love you both very much and I will see you on Sunday," she said and closed the door. She then walked around to the other side of the truck where her husband was waiting. "James, I will miss you guys so much, but I want you to have fun and I will see you when you get back," she said as she leaned in and kissed him.

"I love you too. I will see you on Sunday," he replied as he started up the truck. "I will try to call you later, but I am not sure if we will have reception by the lake. The mountains sometimes block reception."

"I know, hon, have a great time," she said as James began backing down the driveway and then into the dirt road.

CHAPTER

FIVE

A "PENNY" FOR

YOUR THOUGHTS

Courtney entered the house, feeling the emptiness. This was the first time that her whole family went away without her. She was glad for the peace and quiet. She would get some of her book written, but she was going to have a hard time sleeping at night without James, and the thought of not putting her sons to bed for two nights was more than she could take. Courtney sat down in the chair and cried. She cried over missing her family, and the results she had gotten earlier that day. After about ten minutes, she got up and went to the kitchen. She grabbed a glass of wine, and headed up to the office.

James' wife sat down at the computer and turned it on. She waited for it to start up and then opened the file that contained her book. She began to type until Mako jumped on her lap, scaring her a bit. "Hi Mako," she said as she pet him on the head. She noticed that he had a few scratches on his back. "What happened to you?" she asked. "You have new scratches," she said as she examined the cats back. Mako let out a cry, as she looked him over. "I am sorry, Mako. I did not mean to hurt you," she said as Mako jumped off of her lap.

Courtney was typing away at her book for hours, completely unaware of the time. She was finally getting some work done, some real progress at her book. Her eyes were getting tired and she was beginning to drift in and out as she was working. Finally she looked at the clock, two thirteen am. "Holy shit, it's late. No wonder I can barely keep my eyes open," she said. Then she saved the file and headed to bed. She had a hard time getting comfortable without James, but she finally drifted off to sleep.

Saturday morning, Courtney awoke at about ten am. she instantly thought she had overslept. "The kids," she said alarmed. Then she realized that she was home alone. She got out of bed, and headed to the shower. She was planning on going to lunch and then back to her book. After her shower, she threw her hair up in a clip and grabbed her keys. She drove to Apple bee's and grabbed a seat at the bar. She ordered herself a tea and a Caesar salad. She talked to a girl that was sitting a few seats down from her. Her name was Jill. Courtney told her about her family being off camping and listened while the woman told her that her ex-husband had her kids for the weekend. The two of them laughed about their lives and talked about their jobs while they ate. Jill was excited to meet a big city children's book writer. Courtney was fascinated to hear that Jill was an orthopedic surgeon. Their conversation was wonderful.

When lunch was over, Courtney and Jill walked out together. Courtney gave Jill a copy of one of her books she had in her car and autographed it for her. "Thank you so much, Courtney for the book," she said.

"You are so welcome. It was nice to meet you," Courtney replied.

Back at the house, Courtney was working hard at her book and she was determined she would finish it today. She was excited about her hard work and the thought that it was done before schedule. She was nearly finished when she realized that she had not moved from the computer for hours. She got up, stretched her legs and looked out the window. It was a beautiful day. The sun was shining and the pool looked inviting. Courtney decided to go for a swim.

With the boys being gone, the swim was short. She was missing her kids and the swim was not the same without them. She got out of the pool and toweled off, went inside and tried to call James. She dialed over and over again with the same results, a voice mail. James did not have reception.

Courtney gave up after about three tries. "It's no use; I can't get him," she said. Courtney went into the bathroom and took off her bathing suit and put on her bath robe. She looked at the clock four eighteen pm. She was glad that most of the day was over. "They'll come home tomorrow," she said to herself and walked into the office, sat back down at her computer and began to type in her book again. Courtney continued to type her book until she was finished.

Satisfied with herself, she smiled, and then saved her work. She then sent an e-mail to her publisher that the book was done with the attached file. She needed to copy it to a disk for her records. Courtney always followed up her work by putting it on a disk, just in case her computer ever crashed on her. Courtney reached down and grabbed the handle of the bottom drawer of her desk and opened it. As she opened it she screamed at what she saw. Courtney jumped up out of her chair. "JAMES! JAMES!" she yelled as she closed the draw. Courtney then realized that James was not there. She then slowly reached her hand down to the draw with tears in her eyes. She really did not want to open it again, but she knew that it had to be done. She trembled in fear as she gripped the handle. "Please, please God, don't let it be what I saw," she said and closed her eyes as she opened the draw.

With her eyes slowly opening, Courtney realized that she was seeing something that she just could not believe. Mako, her beloved cat was curled up in the draw, DEAD. She cried and cried over the sight of her dead cat. "Oh Mako, how did you get in that draw? What happened to you?" she asked as the tears were streaming down her face. "What do I do now?" she questioned. "I can't get in touch with James," she continues. "Mako, I don't know what to do," she cried.

Courtney went downstairs, crying over the loss of her cat. She put on her shoes and went outside in her robe. She went into

the garage and grabbed a shovel, and headed down to the back part of the lawn. Courtney began to dig a hole for her cat.

"What are you doing?" Linda asked.

"Linda, you scared me," Courtney replied. "I am digging a hole," she continued to say as she put down the shovel. "I, my cat, Mako died today," she stuttered as she talked to Linda.

"I know that. I was just wondering why you were burying him here and not by the water," she responded.

"Mako loved to sit in the office window and look out at the

lawn. So I figured that I should bury him in the lawn," she said as she turned to the shovel and began to dig again.

"Why would I bury him by the water?" she asked and turned around to see that Linda was gone.

Back in the house, Courtney took Mako's lifeless body out of the draw and wrapped him in a towel. She carried him down the stairs and placed him on the couch. She then sat on the couch next to him and said a prayer for the safe journey to heaven or where ever pets go. Then she picked up her cat and carried him out to the hole that she dug and laid him in it. "I wish James and the kids were here. I miss them and I really don't want to bury him without them," she stated as she covered the hole with dirt. "How do I tell the boys?" she said as she wiped the tears from her eyes and walked back to the house.

Courtney was a mess. The tears were covering her face to the point that she could no longer see. She picked up her cell phone and tried James again. "Shit, he is out of range. I need to tell the boys what happened to Mako," she said. "How do I let them come home to an empty house and a freshly dug hole?" she asked herself. Courtney needed to make this right for her family. She thought for a while about what to do and then she came up with an idea.

She raced upstairs and threw on a pair of pants and a sweatshirt. She snatched up the keys and headed to the local craft store. She walked inside and found a wooden plaque that she could put Mako's name on and grabbed some paint and brushes, paid for them and left the store. She then stopped at Stewart's, bought the paper and went home.

Once at home, Courtney took the paints out of the bag. She then took a plate out of the cabinet and poured the paint on it. Courtney dipped a brush into the blue paint with a shaking hand.

She had to wipe the tears out of her eyes as she tried to paint the word MAKO on the plaque. She had all she could do to get the word written. She then walked away to let the word dry.

Later that day, Courtney began to look through the paper. She was looking through the classified section for a new cat for her family. She found nothing, nothing that would fill the void that Mako left behind. She then saw an advertisement for the local animal shelter. Courtney was feeling confused about what happened to her cat, and knowing that her boys could not come home to an empty house, she grabbed her keys and headed out the door to the shelter.

Courtney found herself standing in front of the local S.P.C.A. She read the sign that said the hours of operation. "Thank God" she said when she found out that they were still open. She opened the door and walked inside. She could hear the meowing and barking of the homeless animals. Slowly she walked down the hallway toward the section that held the cats. She passed a man and a woman on the way, the couple who were walking with a beautiful golden retriever mix. The dog instantly caught her eye. She watched as they took the dog into the other room. She stopped dead in her tracks and watched through the glass to see if they were going to take the dog. Time stood still as Courtney waited to see what this dog's fate would be. The couple finally opened the door. "Excuse me, are you going to take that dog?' asked Courtney.

"We have decided not to. The technician said that she was a dog that would be good with kids, and we don't have any. We decided it would not be fair to her," the lady stated.

"Could I take a look at her, if you don't mind?" Courtney asked.

"That's fine. We were just going to have them put her back in her cage. She is a really nice dog and I hope it works out for you," she replied.

"Thank you," Courtney stated as she took the leash out of the woman's hand.

Courtney opened the door to the little room where she would get to know the dog. She could see that she had a tag on her collar that read "PENNY." "What a perfect name for you," she said as she began to pet the dog. Penny reached out her paw and put it on Courtney's leg. "Well, aren't you the friendly one," Courtney stated as she took Penny's paw in her hand. "Hold on, girl, I am going to see what the deal is about you.

Out in the main hall, Courtney met up with one of the workers. "Can you tell me anything about this dog Penny?" she asked.

"Penny was a dog that was saved when a family moved away and for some reason, they left her behind. She is the sweetest tempered dog and she loves children. She should have been placed in a home by now, but she was sick and just got put up for adoption today. I don't expect her to be here long," she said.

"How old is she?" Courtney asked.

"She is just over two years old," the woman responded.

"I want to adopt her," Courtney stated with a smile on her face. "I have two boys who would love to have her as a pet and I have a huge yard and a creek with fresh running water behind the house. I know we could give her a good home," Courtney continued. "She would be so spoiled, and loved," she added.

"Well, let's get the paperwork then," the worker stated. "We will need to see your identification," she continued.

"That's fine, I will go get it out of the car and meet you back in the room with Penny," Courtney stated and headed out to her car.

With all the papers signed, Courtney was able to walk out the front door with Penny, the newest addition to the Stealth family. She opened the passenger side door and Penny climbed in and sat down on the seat. She watched as Courtney walked to the other side, got in and closed the door behind her. "Well, Penny, here is a chance at a new life for you," Courtney stated and patted Penny on the head. Then she started the car and headed for the store.

Courtney cracked the window of the car in the parking lot and walked into the store. She needed to get dog food and treats for her new pet. She was concerned that she did not talk to James about getting the dog, but she was sure that he would be alright with it. They had talked about getting a dog previously. With her pet food in hand, Courtney headed back to the car. She put the supplies on the back seat and got into the driver's seat and started the car. She looked over at Penny who was wagging her tail. "Looks like we are all set here," she said and pet Penny on the back. "Come on Penny, time to get you home."

Penny and Courtney arrived home just before dark. Courtney hooked her up to the brand new leash she purchased and took her for a walk around the side yard so she could get used to the smells. Then the two of them headed for the house. Penny walked inside and began to sniff the rug. She looked up at Courtney and then climbed on the couch and waited to see if it was alright. "It's okay girl," she said to her as she sat down on the couch and put her hand on her back.

As Penny slept on the couch, Courtney went out to the car and brought in her food and treats. She took a bowl out of the cupboard and put it on the floor. She then poured the food into the bowl.

Penny, hearing the food, jumped off the couch, came into the kitchen and began to eat. "Well, that is a good sign that you like it here," Courtney said as she reached down and ran her hand down the dogs back. Then she got out another bowl and filled it with water. Penny stopped eating and watched until Courtney was finished and put the bowl down. Then she began to drink. "Good girl, Penny," Courtney stated and headed back to the couch. Just as Courtney sat down, the cell phone rang. She jumped up to answer it. She could see that it was James calling. "Hello, James. Thank God you called," Courtney said in a panic.

"What's wrong, C.J.?" James asked.

"Oh James, Mako died today. He was in the desk draw and I have no idea how he got there. I was so upset, but I managed to bury him. Please don't tell the boys until you get home. I don't want to ruin their trip,"

"Courtney, are you okay? Do you want us to come home now?" he asked.

"No, James, don't come home. Have fun with the boys. James, I was so upset that I decided to get a dog. Are you mad at me?" she asked.

"No hon, I am not mad, hold on," he stated. Then there was a pause. "Okay C.J. I am away from the boys now so what kind of dog did you get?" he asked.

"Well I went to the S.P.C.A. Looking for a cat and this beautiful lab mix won my heart over. Her name is Penny, James, and she has a copper colored coat. She is super friendly and lovable. I think the kids are going to love her. How are the kids anyway? I miss them so much."

"The boys are fine. They are having a great time. We just

came down to the village of Lake George for dinner. That is why I have reception," he stated. "I can't wait to meet the new dog, and Courtney, I really wish I was there to help you with Mako," James continued. "I know how much he meant to you, to all of us." He told his wife that he loved her and he needed to get back to the table. The boys were finished with dinner and waiting for him to get back to camp.

"Okay James, I will see you tomorrow. I love you and tell the boys I love them too," she said.

"I will, we love you too," he replied and hung up the phone.

"Well, Penny," Courtney stated as she put the phone down. It is just you and me for tonight, but tomorrow you get to meet the rest of your family," she said as she sat on the couch and patted the cushion next to her so the dog would sit by her.

Penny and Courtney both fell asleep on the couch. Courtney was exhausted from her ordeal with Mako and fell to sleep in front of the television petting her new friend. She could not bring herself to go upstairs where she had found Mako, so falling asleep on the couch was the best thing for her. She woke once in the night when Penny barked, but then fell back to sleep. Courtney figured Penny was getting used to her new home when something in the night startled her. Courtney reached over and calmed the dog down and they both went back to sleep. Courtney was happy to hear her bark. She knew that Penny would protect the family if anyone broke into the house during the night.

The next morning, Courtney awoke to find Penny curled up on the floor next to the couch. She was sound asleep, snoring away until she heard Courtney get up. "Well, good morning girl," she stated as she reached down as pat the dog on the head. "I think it is a beautiful morning and I would love to take you for a walk," Courtney continued. "Just let me get dressed and we can walk to the corner," she finished.

Courtney went upstairs and got dressed. She tossed her hair in a pony tail and put a hat on her head. She came back down the stairs to see that Penny was eating in the kitchen. "You must really like it here girl," Courtney stated as she grabbed the dog's leash off the coffee table. "You want to go?" she asked. Penny saw the leash and came running, wagging her tail and sat at Courtney's feet. "I am telling you that someone taught you well," she stated as she put the leash on her.

Penny and Courtney walked down the road with Penny sniffing every inch of her new surroundings. Courtney watched her carefully to see how she acted around other animals and moving vehicles. She was very impressed with her calm nature. Not once did she try to drag Courtney or take off when she saw a squirrel that ran out in front of them. She had picked a good dog for her family. She just hoped that the boys were going to be able to deal with the death of Mako.

Back at the house, Courtney took Penny upstairs to check out the rest of the house. She showed her the boy's rooms and the toy room, with her sniffing every inch of each room. She then took her into the master bedroom when Penny instantly went into the office and barked at the drop stairs for the attic. "Penny, it is just the attic," Courtney stated and patted the dog on the head. Penny instantly calmed down when she felt Courtney's touch. She then climbed upon the spare bed and lay down. "So is this going to be your new bed, girl?" Courtney asked with a smile on her face and sat down next to her. "You know what, Pen?" she stated. "I saw some old furniture up in the attic when we first moved in. Maybe I should take a look again," she said. Then remembered the gigantic spider she saw. "Never mind I will wait until James is home to do that," she stated with a smile on her face.

As Courtney sat petting the dog, she could hear a truck coming down the dirt road. Not just any truck, but James' truck. "It's your new family, Penny. You get to meet your new family," Courtney said getting up off the bed. "Come, Penny," she said and Penny jumped off the bed with a wagging tail.

Courtney was standing on the porch when James pulled into the driveway. She had left Penny in the house so she could surprise the boys. She was so excited to see her family. It had only been a few days, but it was a rough few days for Courtney. "James," she called. "I missed you and the boys so much," Billy was the first one in Courtney's arms.

"Mommy, I missed you so much," he said as he kissed his mother's cheek. Then Andy was standing on the porch.

"I want to hug Mom too; let me have a turn," he stated as Billy moved out of the way. "Mom, we had so much fun," Andy said as he hugged his mom. "We went fishing and I caught the biggest fish. Billy touched a worm too, Mom," Andy said as he let go of his mom.

"Wow, sounds like you guys had fun," she said as she grabbed the door knob to the front door. "I have something to tell you when Daddy gets up here," she stated as she let go of the door knob. "I want you to wait here until he unloads the stuff from the truck.

James had finished unloading the truck and walked up on the porch. "Hi hon," he said and kissed his wife. "Why are we waiting out here?" he asked.

"Well, I figured I should tell the boys about out new friend and about Mako,"Courtney responded.

"What about Mako?" Andy asked.

"Well, Mako passed away this weekend when you guys were

camping," Courtney stated as she got to her knees to talk face to face with her boys. "I am not sure what he died of, but I buried him in the yard," she continued to say. Billy began to cry and Andy just climbed into his father's arms. "I know you guys are sad," Courtney stated and hugged Billy, but I did get you a new friend. Her name is Penny and she is waiting for you in the house."

"I don't want a new cat," Billy said crying and wiping the tears from his face.

"I never said it was a cat," Courtney said and got back up and opened the front door.

Penny, the beautiful lab mix, was sitting in the front door wagging her tail. She was waiting for her new family to come in and see her. She got one look at Billy and went right to him on the porch and began to lick the tears off his face. She then went to James, who was still holding Andy, and gently put her front paws up on his leg and licked Andy's pant leg. Then got back down and sat at James' feet and wagged her tail.

"Mom, she is beautiful," Billy stated and walked over and hugged his new dog. Andy climbed down from his father's arms and pet Penny on the head.

"Where did you bury Mako, Mom?" Andy asked.

"He is in the corner of the yard, just before the path to the creek," she responded.

"Can I go see him?" Andy asked.

"Sure, we can all go over and see where he is buried," she said. "Let me get Penny's leash and we can go," she continued.

The family walked over to where Mako was buried. James walked with Penny and Courtney held hands with her boys.

"Mommy, do you think that Mako was in pain before he died?" Billy asked.

"No, I am sure that he was sleeping and just passed away," Courtney replied.

"Can I have a picture of him to put in my room?" Andy asked.

"Me too," Billy added.

"I will give you both a picture of Mako to keep in your rooms. I promise that I will print them tonight before you go to bed," Courtney responded.

James, Courtney, and the boys were cleaning up the camping gear and unloading the coolers. They could see that Penny was behaving very well on her lead, so they decided to let her off and see what she would do. Just as they thought, she stayed right with them. She followed them to the garage and lay down in the driveway as they cleaned the garbage out of the truck.

"She really is a good dog, C.J," James said and kissed his wife. "I missed you so much and I wish I was here to help you with Mako. I am sure that was a very rough thing for you to do," he continued.

"It was horrible, James. I needed you, but I did what needed to be done so the boys did not come home to see him like that," she stated.

"I know, Courtney, I know," James said putting away everything. "Come, Penny," James called.

The Stealth family had dinner in front of the television that evening. They cleaned out the left over hot dogs and food from the cooler. Then the boys and James all took showers and the family settled down and watched a movie with Penny lying on the floor between the two boys. Courtney was sitting on the couch with James laying his head on her lap. It was a quiet Sunday night, the kind one has when you had a long weekend and all you want to do is relax.

CHAPTER

SIX

THE ATTIC

(Part one)

Courtney was sitting at her desk. The boys were in school
and James was at work. She was busy writing a new short story for
the New York Times, a request from her publisher. Penny was
sleeping on the spare bed. Courtney noticed that the time was two
fourteen pm., exactly one minute before the time that she lately
noticed Penny barking every day. She stopped typing and looked at
the dog. Sure enough, Penny barked at the ceiling. "What is it with
you, Pen? What do you hear, or what do you know that I don't
know?" Courtney asked. "It has been like this since I brought you

home. What is it about that attic?" she asked as she pet Penny on the back of her neck. "Well, girl, one of these days I am going to go up in that attic. You know that there is a spider up there," she said with a smile. "Okay girl, let go get the boys off the bus.

Penny walked with Courtney down to the bus stop for the last three days including today, without missing a beat. She loved to see her boys getting off the bus. Penny had been with the family for five days now, with no problems or complaints. She did have her daily barking spell, which James has not heard yet and questions Courtney of its existence. She had become Courtney's "side kick," as James would say.

Penny and Courtney met the boys at the bus stop, as they had the past few days. Penny covered them both with kisses and wagged her tail all the way home. For the past few days, she went to the kitchen and sat in front of the sink. She knew that the boys were going to give her a cookie from the cupboard. It had become a habit for her that she loved. Then it was play time for Penny until mom called the boys for dinner. Penny loved her afternoon with the boys.

Friday morning, Courtney said goodbye to James, put the boys on the bus and came back to the house with Penny. The two of them went up to the office. Courtney had told James again about Penny's barking spell at two fifteen every day and he thought she was just making it up. She was determined today to get into the attic. "Well Pen, let's see what all the fuss is about," she said, as she grabbed the chain to the attic stairs.

Courtney pulled the stairs down and began to climb. She looked at both sides to see if there was a spider and then finished climbing the ladder. Penny began to bark the second Courtney's foot hit the top step. "What is it, girl? Why are you barking?" Courtney asked as she looked back down the stairs. "I'm alright, just looking around a bit up here. Courtney walked further into the attic. She could see that there was sheet covered furniture everywhere and boxes of old memories of days gone by in this house. "Why would anyone leave all this stuff behind?" she questioned. She walked over to a white sheet that covered a couch and pulled it off. Dust flew everywhere and Courtney began to sneeze. She waved her hand in front of her face to clear the dust then looked at the couch in front of her. "Wow, that is one old couch," she stated with a grin. "It looks like it is straight out of the forty's. The couch in question was covered in a large floral pattern with a wooden back. It was in excellent shape with no tear marks or stains. It had a small dent in the wooden arm, as if someone had dropped something hard on it.

Courtney decided to open a small window in the back of the attic. She wanted to air out the dust. She walked over to the window and opened it. She looked out at the back yard, and she could see right to the creek. The leaves on the trees were turning and falling to the ground. She took a closer look and thought she saw someone walking. "Hey, who's out there?" she yelled. Then the image was gone. Courtney rubbed her eyes and looked again. "I am seeing things again," she said to herself.

With the window open and fresh air coming in, Courtney was beginning to feel better. She continued to look around at all the boxes and covered furniture. She had no idea how they were going to get this attic cleared of all the old furniture and boxes. There was much more stuff here than she thought when they first moved in. Courtney decided that this project was a bit too big for her. She was going to wait for James, so she headed back down the stairs to Penny who was waiting for her with a wagging tail. "Well Penny, there is nothing too scary up there, so you can stop barking," she said and kissed her on her nose. Then Courtney closed up the attic and headed down the stairs with Penny and went for a walk.

Upon their return, Courtney cleaned the house. She did laundry and dishes and ran the vacuum, which always scared Penny. She did not mean to scare the dog, but for some reason Penny hated that vacuum. When she was finished, she went upstairs and worked on her article for the paper while she waited for the boys to come home. Right at 2:15 pm. Penny barked, looking at the ceiling. "I don't know what is going on with you Pen. I wonder if something happened to you at this particular time," Courtney stated and got up and hugged her dog. Then the two of them went to the bus stop to get the boys, just like they did every other day.

That evening, at the dinner table, James and Courtney discussed how they were going to plan Billy's party. They decided that they were going to have a pool party the following weekend. "I need to get the names of all your friends so I can write up the invitations and send them in to school," Courtney said as she cleared the dinner table. "I will get them from your school site on the computer," Courtney continued. "I will call Grandma Brenda and Grandma Marge and make sure that they are coming too."

CHAPTER

SEVEN

THE PARTY

The house was covered in streamers, inside and out. There was a HAPPY BIRTHDAY banner taped to the railing on the front porch and balloons everywhere. The guests were beginning to arrive and Billy was ecstatic. Grandma Brenda was sitting on the porch drinking a cup of tea and Grandma Marge was in the kitchen helping her daughter get the refreshments to bring them out to the pool. James was instructing the guest to head to the pool, where Billy was waiting with his brother Andy.

With all the guests enjoying themselves, James started up the grill and began to cook. Courtney was bringing the salads that she made out to the picnic table while her mother was gathering up the cups, napkins, and plasticware that they would need and brought them to the table. Courtney went back in the house to get the rolls. "Hi Courtney," Linda said from the kitchen.

"Well hello Linda. How are you?" Courtney replied as she walked into the kitchen. Courtney could not help but notice that Linda was wearing the same dress she wore every time she saw her. She was beginning to think that her parents did not even care about her appearance. "Linda, why do you wear the same dress all the time?" Courtney asked.

"I, well, never mind that," Linda said as she grabbed her by the arm. "Come play with me!" she demanded.

"I can't play with you right now; I have my son's birthday party going on. Why don't you come and join the party. I would have invited you earlier, but I have not seen you," Courtney replied.

"No! No party. Come upstairs and play with me. I have never played with anyone else but, never mind. It was not fun. Now let's go!" she screamed as she tried to pull Courtney with her.

"Linda, I have guests and I am not going with you!' Courtney replied very sternly and removed Linda's hand from her arm.

"Fine," Linda stated and crossed her arms. "You will play with me some day. I will make sure of that!" she stated and ran to the living room and up the stairs. Courtney was confused, but ran after her to see where she was going.

"Linda," she called as she got to the top of the stairs. "Linda, where are you?" she called as she entered Andy's room. "Are you in here?" she asked. Then she looked in the toy room and Billy's room to no avail. "Maybe she is in my room," Courtney stated as she headed to her bedroom. Courtney looked under the bed and in the closet, and then entered the office. Linda was sitting on the spare bed, with her hands covering her face. She was crying and talking out loud.

"I wouldn't play with me either if I were you. I would not want them to hurt you for playing with me, after what happened to Mako. I just figured that you would be nice to me and fun to play with," she cried.

As Courtney approached Linda, to help comfort her, the picture of Mako and the boys fell off the wall. Linda stood up on the bed and screamed. "I can't stay here; they won't let me! Courtney, I needed your help, but they won't let me talk to you anymore! I have to go! I, they, they are here now!" She screamed, then ran past Courtney and down the stairs slamming the front door. Courtney realized that Linda was gone.

Courtney could hear James calling her from outside. She went to the window and James waved for her to come outside. "I'm coming. I'll be right there!" she yelled, then picked up the picture and set it on the desk. She walked down the stairs and back to the party.

James was at the grill, and Courtney could see that all the guests were having a blast. She approached James and said "James, Linda was just in the house." She was acting a bit weird and took off upstairs into the office," she whispered. "She said something about the last people that she played with hurt her somehow. She mentioned Mako then a picture fell off the wall, and she was gone," Courtney stated.

"What are you talking about?" James asked.

"Linda was here, here at the house," Courtney responded.

"I heard you, but what about Mako?" James asked.

"I don't know what she was saying James. I just know that she was scared and she mentioned playing with someone who hurt her," Courtney said.

"Courtney, I don't know what to tell you. She probably comes from a bad home, I think, and until you find out what she is talking about, there is nothing we can do for her," James said. "Anyway, the guests are waiting for cake and Billy wants to open presents.

"Okay, I will go get the cake," Courtney stated and walked toward the house.

Billy was waiting at the picnic table with a huge smile on his face. He was watching and waiting as the family and his friends were singing happy birthday to him. He was so excited to have almost half of his classmates at his house. He never figured he would have so many friends turn out for his party. Billy blew out the candles on his cake and helped his mother pass out slices and ice cream. They all sat around at the table and in lawn chairs and ate their cake as Billy began opening his presents. He was halfway through when he got to a present from Grandma Brenda. He opened it and saw that she had gotten him a Nintendo D.S. "Grandma! He yelled and got up from his chair. "You're the best! This is what I wanted."

"You are very welcome," she said and hugged her grandson. "Well if you like that, you may want to open Grandma Marge's gift, too," Brenda stated as she sat back down in her chair.

"I will," Billy stated and pawed his way through the gifts until he found her present. Billy opened it to see that Grandma Marge had gotten him four different games for his new D.S. system. "Thank you so much," Billy said and jumped into her arms. "I have the two best Grandmothers in the world!" he yelled and went over to the table and finished opening his gifts.

When the party was over, and the guests were gone, Grandma Brenda helped Billy open his D.S. He then kissed her and said goodbye to Grandma Marge, and headed to the toy room with Andy to take turns playing his new game. James had gone outside to Brenda's car and got her bags and put them in the office. Courtney was right behind him getting ready to say goodbye to her mother.

"Mom," she said. "Please be careful driving home and call when you get there," she said and opened the car door for her.

"I will, I promise," she replied and got in the car.

"Alright, Mom, I love you and I will talk to you soon," Courtney said and leaned in the window and kissed her mother on the cheek.

It was about nine pm. when Marge called. She had made it home. She thanked her daughter for a wonderful party. "Thank Brenda for coming up with the perfect gift for us to give to our grandson."

"I will, Mom. I love you and I will talk to you soon," Courtney stated.

"I love you too," Marge replied and hung up the phone.

Courtney and James went upstairs to put the boys to bed. Brenda had already turned in for the night. She laughed when she did, because she had to get Penny off her bed in order to get into it. With the boys tucked in, and Brenda in bed, the couple sat down and talked about the day's events. Courtney brought it to James'

attention that Penny probably barked at the attic door today, but
with the party, no one heard her. She also talked to him about
Linda and what had happened. "I am sure you are overreacting,
Courtney."

"No James, I am not!" she said sternly. "She was wearing the
same dress, and she was acting weird. She really wanted me to
play with her and then when she ran upstairs, she was scared to
death," Courtney stated. "There is something wrong with that
child, James, and I am going to figure it out," she continued. "Like
why does she never come around when you are here?" or why does
she always want me to play? She never says what we are going to
play, just play, it is like it is something she is ordering me to do
and not asking me," she said with a confused look on her face.

"I don't have any answers," James said and put his arm around
his wife. "I wish I did C.J, I really wish I did."

Later that evening, James and Courtney settled in for the
night. They had both taken a shower and they were off to bed.
Courtney stopped long enough to check on her kids and make sure
that Brenda was doing alright. She could see that Penny was next
to her feet, snoring. The couple then curled up next to each other
and watched television in bed until Courtney drifted off to sleep.
James then turned the television off and kissed his wife on the
cheek, rolled over and fell asleep himself.

The next day, Brenda and Courtney were in the kitchen
making breakfast for the family. James and the kids were in the toy
room playing with all of Billy's new birthday presents. Penny was
lying on the floor waiting for Brenda and Courtney to drop some
food for her. The family was having a wonderful morning. With
breakfast made, Courtney called the boys and James to the kitchen.
The family sat at the kitchen table with their grandmother and
enjoyed their eggs, bacon and pancakes. Grandma Brenda asked

Billy about his upcoming party at her house. She wanted to know what he wanted for decorations and who he wanted her to invite. They decided to have a basic backyard party.brenda would get a few games together and set up water balloon tag and other games to play. The party was going to be the following weekend, so Courtney and Billy made a list of friends for Brenda to invite.

With breakfast finished, and the table cleaned up, Brenda decided to go take a shower and get ready for her long trip home. She went to the office and gathered the things she needed from the suitcase. She went into the bathroom to find a clump of long blonde curly hair in the sink. The hair didn't belong to anyone in that house. She just knew. The whole family had brown hair. "Must be from the party, one of Billy's friends," and she tossed the hair in the garbage can next to the toilet. Brenda was packed and ready to go. It was just before two o'clock pm. Courtney wanted her to stay a bit longer so she could observe the dog reactions at two fifteen. She also wanted to make sure that James was upstairs to hear the dog bark at the ceiling, but he was saying goodbye to his mother. So, Courtney was unable to get anyone to see what she was seeing and hear what she was hearing. She was tired of everyone thinking she was crazy. The family waved goodbye to grandma and watched her leave down the dirt road. The boys then went back to the house to play with the gold mine of toys that Billy just received and James headed out to the garage to finish cleaning up from the party yesterday. Courtney looked at her watch and realized that it was only seven minutes after two. "James, James wait. Will you please come upstairs with me and see what this dog does?" Courtney asked. James walked back to his wife and gently put his hands on both sides of her face.

"C.J., I am not going to feed into this. The dog is fine. There is nothing going on with her. She just barks sometimes. The thought that she barks at the same time every day is crazy," he said.

"James, she," Courtney began to say, but James had put his finger over her mouth and told her to stop. He then walked away back to the garage shaking his head and talking to himself about what his wife was saying. "Fine, James!" Courtney yelled across the driveway. "Don't believe me, I don't care. I know that I am not crazy!" she continues. "You will see, one of these days, you will be in this house and you will hear her!" she yelled and slammed the door behind her.

Courtney went to the downstairs bathroom and began to clean it. It was quite dirty after the party yesterday. She was just about to sweep the floor when she heard Penny barking. Courtney dropped the broom. "That's it, someone else is going to know about this!" she demanded. She walked up the stairs to the toy room. "Boys, do you hear that? Do you hear your dog?" She asked almost yelling at them.

"Yes, Mom," Andy responded.

"I hear her, too" Billy stated.

"Look at the clock; look at it!" she yelled. "Tell me what time it is!" "Tell me!"

"Mom, it is two fifteen. Why are you yelling at us?" Andy asked. Courtney stopped dead in her tracks, dropped to the floor and began to cry. "I am so sorry, both of you. I never meant to yell at you. It's just Penny, every day this week, she has barked at this time of day and I can't figure it out," she continued crying. Billy hugged his mom and kissed her.

"Please don't cry, Mom." Andy said.

Courtney wiped the tears from her eyes and stood back up.

"I'm sorry, I am. I just overreacted and I am so sorry I yelled at the two of you," she stated and walked out of the toy room. She then went into the bathroom to get a tissue. She wiped the tears from her face, and went to toss the tissue in the garbage.

There it was, what Courtney believed was proof. She saw in the garbage can a large lock of golden yellow hair. Courtney picked it up out of the garbage. "What do I do? Should I tell James? No, he won't believe me," she said and slipped the lock of hair into her pocket. She then left the bathroom and went into to office where Penny was sleeping soundly on the bed. "Well, girl, you and I are going to figure this out together," she said as she sat down next to the dog. "The minute the kids are gone, I am going to start figuring this mess out. Who is here? What is she trying to tell me? Who are THEY?" she asked as if the dog was going to have the answers. "All I know is that little girl needs my help and I am NOT going to let her down!" she stated with confidence as she got up and went back to cleaning the bathroom.

James and Courtney ate dinner in silence. The boys could tell that their parents were not getting along. They finished their meal and went outside to play. Later that evening, Courtney and James tucked the boys in bed and James watched TV as Courtney went into the office to print out pictures of Mako. She was crying because James had never treated her like this before. He always supported her no matter what she was doing. But now, now he was pulling away and she hated that feeling.

The whole Stealth family was in bed. Courtney was the only one who was awake. She was holding onto Linda's hair, tight in her hand. She was thinking about how she could find this little girl and help her. Somehow she had to help find out who "THEY" were, and what they had done to her. She was beginning to feel tired, so she reached over and opened the night stand and placed Linda's lock of hair in the draw. For the first time in a very long time, she rolled away from James and fell asleep.

CHAPTER

EIGHT

THE ATTIC

(Part two)

Courtney awoke at about five am. She reached over and grabbed the lock of hair out of the drawer. She got up and put on her robe and headed downstairs to get James' lunch made. She called Penny to come with her and then let her outside. She got out the luncheon meat and was making James' lunch when she heard Penny barking. She set down the sandwich and went to the front door. "What is it, Penny?" she asked as Penny continued to bark. "What's the matter, girl?" she continued as she walked out the front door onto the porch. Courtney stood next to Penny and looked around the corner of the house to the side porch. She could see a shadow of a person on the side of the house, but there appeared to be no one there.

The shadow was about six feet tall with broad shoulders. It was along the side of the house where the window at the base of the stairs was. Courtney slowly approached to see if she could find the person who cast the shadow. As she got closer, she heard these words. "Get out of my house." Then the shadow was gone. Courtney stepped back in fear and looked around. Feeling a bit scared, she ran back to the front door.

"Come, Penny!" she yelled as she waited for her dog. Inside the house, Courtney could hear the water running. She ran up the stairs to the bathroom and opened the door. "James," she called. "James, I saw someone's shadow outside. There was someone on the porch," she continued. "Someone's shadow was shining on the side of the house." James opened the shower door.

"Hand me a towel and I will go check it out," he stated as he put his hand outside the shower curtain.

James and Courtney went outside on the porch. James asked Courtney where she saw the person. "Well, it was not a person, just the shadow of a person, and then it spoke. The shadow told me to get out of the house. "Are you kidding me, Courtney? A shadow, that's all you saw? It could have been anything, a tree shadow, the clouds," James stated as he pointed to both. "And to hear someone talking?"

"Yes, James, I heard someone, I know you don't believe me, you never do!" Courtney screamed.

"Now that is not fair. I did not say I did not believe you," James said and took Courtney by the hand. I am just saying that what you saw could have been anything."

"Look James," Courtney began. "I saw what I saw, and heard what I heard, no matter what you believe," and Courtney walked back to the front door. "I'm going to get your lunch made so you are not late for work. I suggest you get ready. Come, Penny," she stated while she walked in the door with the dog and back into the kitchen.

James went back in the house and upstairs, got dressed for work and came back down. He went to the kitchen to get his lunch from Courtney. "Listen C.J., I think you should go see someone about this. You are acting so weird, seeing and hearing things that are not real. I am worried about you," James stated.

"Look James, I already saw a doctor the other day. I am fine. There is nothing wrong with me except that my own husband does not believe me anymore," she said and shoved his lunch into his hand and walked past him and headed upstairs to get the boys up for school.

James came to the bottom of the stairs. "C.J., I'm sorry, I don't know what is going on with us, but I am sorry for my part. I love you and I will see you after work," he stated and turned and walked out the front door, leaving Courtney to deal with what he just said. All she could do is shake her head and continue to get the boys ready for school.

It was a rainy Monday. There was no walking to the bus stop, so Courtney loaded the boys into the car with Penny and drove to the bus stop. The bus came and then she took Penny down the road to the store. She needed to get milk and figured she should go now because when she got home, she was going to look for answers. She walked into the store and grabbed some milk and headed back to the house. She tossed some chicken in the crock pot with salsa, and headed upstairs.

Courtney pulled down the stairs of the attic with Penny by her feet. She slowly climbed the ladder, step by step. As soon as she hit the top step, Penny started barking. "It's okay, girl," she said and continued into the attic. "I know I saw something, someone on that porch, and I will find out whom," she said to herself as she continued on.

Courtney picked up one of the boxes and set it on the couch she uncovered the other day. She then opened the box. The box held clothing that looked like they were from the early fifty's, including old fashioned button up shirts and wool sweaters. She took out a few article of clothing and really looked at them. "I bet these are from the last owners of this house," she said and put the opened box back on the floor. Courtney then grabbed another box.

As Courtney put the box on the couch she heard "GET OUT." Penny began to bark as she ran to the stairs. Courtney stopped only to grab the picture from the floor, a picture of a couple. She tossed it down the stairway to the spare bed on the right of the stairs. She then turned around and climbed down the stairs and closed the attic behind her. She went to the spare bed and grabbed the picture. Penny was sitting on the floor, barking at the attic. Courtney picked up the picture, and went over and patted Penny on the head. "It's alright, girl," she said and then walked away from her and headed down the stairs to get something to clean the glass off with. Courtney grabbed the glass cleaner out from under the kitchen sink and grabbed the paper towels. She went into the living room and sat on the floor. She sprayed the glass with cleaner, and wiped it with the paper towels.

Courtney watched as the picture became clearer. She could see that the picture was a couple in their late forties, standing in front of the house. The house was a bit different, but it was this house, Courtney and James' home. The man in the picture was dressed in bell bottom corduroy pants and a buttoned down striped shirt. He had short brown hair and wore glasses. He was standing with his arm around a short woman who was wearing a brown pair of slacks and she had a beehive hair style. They looked like they were a happy couple, but pictures did not always tell the truth, as Courtney would find out later on.

She took the frame and turned it over. She opened the back of the frame and took the picture out. She turned it over to see if anything was written on the back. She could make out one of the names. It read Joseph P. Wells. The other name she had a hard time with. She could make out a few of the letters, "ebecc." It looked like the first name was Rebecca, and the middle initial was not legible. She could see a few letters of the last name, "Wel." She was sure that it stood for Wells. "So that is who owned this house, and who just told me to get out," she said. "Well, I am not going anywhere! Not until I get answers!" she continued to yell, looking at the ceiling. She then got back up off the floor and tossed the frame on the dining room table and put the picture on the table next to it. She grabbed her coat and her keys and picked up the picture and headed out to her car. She needed answers and she needed them now.

Courtney drove to the local library, the one she saw the other day. She walked inside and headed to the microfiche in the back. She wanted to look up information related to the picture and she wanted it now. She wanted to prove to herself and her husband that she was not crazy. She was hearing things in that house and seeing things as well. She sat at the machine for a few seconds before she realized that she had no clue where to start. She went to the front desk. "Excuse me," she said. "I am looking for some information about the people in this picture. I think it is from the sixties. I was hoping that I could find something here to help me," she said and handed the picture to the librarian.

"Let's see what we can do," the librarian said and looked at the back of the photo. "I think I can help you. I think I know this couple," the elderly lady said. "Did they live out on Beacon Road?" she asked.

"Yes, yes they did," Courtney stated.

"Well, if I remember correctly, it was back in 1962 or 1963, when it happened," the librarian said.

"What happened?" Courtney asked excitedly.

"Well, from what I remember, the husband went crazy. Out of nowhere, he killed his wife. Shot her, I think. Then he shot himself," she stated. "Everyone in town thought he was a bit off, but never figured that he was capable of killing his wife," she replied.

"How do you know so much; did you live around here back then?" Courtney asked.

"I lived right down the road from them with my family. Back then I was about seventeen, just getting ready to graduate from high school. It was all over the news. The whole town was in an uproar," she continued. "By the way, my name is April. Why the interest in the Wells?" she asked.

"April, it is nice to meet you. My interest is with the house. My husband and I bought their house about a month or so ago and I just needed some information. "Is there anything else you can tell me about the couple?" Courtney asked.

"Let's see. They married young. Never did have any kids of their own. He was the quiet type. The talk of the town was that he was abusive to his wife, but there was no proof. I really don't remember much else. I was young and only really knew what people were saying on the news after their deaths," April continued. "If you really want more information, you could look up the old newspapers and reports.

"Thank you for talking with me," Courtney stated.

Armed with the knowledge of the couple, and feeling better about herself, Courtney left the library and headed home. She knew that she needed to get back in that attic and find out more and more information about this couple, a way to reclaim her house and her life. She also wanted to have her husband believe her. For the first time since this started, she felt she could get him to actually believe her. Believe that she was not hearing things but getting messages from a couple who wanted them out of their house, the Wells house.

Courtney went back home. She let the dog out and headed upstairs. She turned on her computer and then went back down to get the dog. She grabbed herself some lunch and took out the pork chops for dinner. Then she headed back up to her desk and sat down. She placed the picture into her scanner and scanned it into her computer. She wanted to save the picture to her documents. Then she went on the internet trying to find information about the house and what had happened. She was surfing the net, but most sites were pay sites. Courtney was getting frustrated. "Why can't I find what I am looking for?" she said and continued searching the net.

Feeling that she exhausted her internet search, she got up from the computer and decided to get some of the housework done. She went downstairs and began to vacuum the living room and dining room. She then went in and swept and mopped the kitchen floor. She was headed to the bathroom when she heard Penny begin to bark. Right on cue, she barked two fifteen pm. "This has got to stop!" she yelled. "Someone has to believe me and hear this dog barking! She continued as she walked out of the bathroom. "Penny," she called. "Penny, come!" she yelled and Penny appeared at the top of the stairs. "Penny, come," Courtney called again. Penny just stood there looking at Courtney. "Pen, are you okay?" Courtney asked as she started to walk up the stairs. Penny just turned and went back into Courtney's room. "Penny?" Courtney almost questioned. "Penny, are you okay?" she asked as she entered the bedroom. "Penny, come," Courtney called again in hope that Penny would come out of the office so Courtney did not have to go in the room. She could feel that something was not right.

Courtney rounded the corner to the office. She could see Penny staring at the spare bed. She looked past Penny to see a pool of blood stained into the comforter. "Penny!" Courtney yelled and ran to the dog. "Are you hurt, are you bleeding?" she asked almost in hysterics. Courtney could feel that Penny was fine. "Where is this blood from?" she said out loud and then she felt the bed. The blood on the comforter was dry. "What the hell is going on here?" Courtney said and grabbed Penny by the collar. "Come, girl, we have to go get the boys," she said as she walked backward out of the room, not taking her eyes off the bed until she was around the corner. Courtney could feel that this house was trying to tell her something, "THEY" were trying to tell her something. All she knew was that she was not leaving, no matter how often "they" told her to. She was going to find away to take back her house, permanently.

Billy, Andy, Courtney and Penny, were back from the bus stop. The boys were in the yard playing with Penny, with Courtney sitting on a lawn chair trying to figure out how to try to talk to James' about the couple who used to live in their house. She was sure that he was not going to want to hear it, but she had evidence this time, the blood on the bed, a blood stain that she did not cause and he had to accept that.

James arrived home that evening about six o'clock. Dinner was almost ready and the boys were washing their hands. Courtney met James at the front door with the picture in her hand. "Look,

James, I found this picture in the attic today. While I was up there, I heard someone tell me to get out."

"Courtney, look. I just got home; I really don't want to hear about the house talking to you right now. Let's have dinner. Then we can talk about this picture. Please C.J., I am tired and hungry," James stated to his wife as he walked passed her and set his keys on the kitchen counter.

"Fine, James, but I really have something important we need to talk about and something to show you," she replied and went and set the table.

The family sat at the dinner table and talked about the boy's day at school and the upcoming soccer practice and, of course, Billy's party in the city. They also discussed James' day at work. The whole time, Courtney was sitting at the table just waiting, waiting for her chance to tell James what she found out and to prove to him, that she was not crazy, that their house actually was haunted.

With the boys in the kitchen doing homework, Courtney brought James to the front porch. She showed him the picture of the couple.

"Okay, I see that they used to live here," he stated.

"Turn it over, James," Courtney said. "Turn it over and read the names." James turned the picture over. He could read the name Joseph P. Wells and another. "So this is the couple that used to own this house?"

"Yes, James," Courtney said. "I was in the attic and I was looking around. I heard someone tell me to get out. I know you don't believe that, but it did happen. I took the picture to the library to look up information on the microfiche. I had no idea how to use it, so the librarian, April, told me that Joseph Wells went crazy. He went crazy, James, and killed his wife, and then himself," she continued.

"Okay C.J., I get it. The couple in this picture is dead. You are hearing things and now what? What do you want me to say? They are dead, C.J.; they are dead. They are not here, not talking to you," he stated and reached out to touch his wife's cheek.

"I knew you would not believe me!" she yelled. "James, I can prove that something is going on in this house," she continued. "Come up to the office. You will see; you will see proof that something is wrong with this house."

James followed Courtney back into the house. Then the two of them headed up the stairs to the office. Courtney walked around the corner, and of course, the stain was gone. "What the hell? She yelled. "James, I swear to God that the comforter was covered in blood."

"C.J., I don't know what is happening to you, but I don't think you should be left alone anymore. I am calling your mom to see if she can stay with you until Saturday," James stated.

"NO! No, James, I am fine. It is this house. The owners don't want us here. Please, James, listen to me. Remember the writing on the wall in Billy's room, the television changing channels, the shadow on the wall, and the person in the rainstorm. Now, there is this," Courtney said. "How can you not believe me, James?" I am not crazy!" Courtney said screaming at her husband.

"Calm down C.J., or the boys are going to hear you," James said calmly to his wife and reached his hand out to her.

"NO!" she yelled. "I will not calm down; I can't even talk to you anymore!" I don't get it James, why do you think I would lie to you?" she screamed.

"It's not that I think you are lying," he said calmly. "I think you are confused, that's all," he said.

"I'm confused, confused about what? I see what I see and I hear what I hear! I can't help that you are not here when it happens. James, just because you are not here does not mean that it is not happening, James!" Courtney yelled and stormed out of the bedroom and down the stairs. She grabbed her keys and told the boys that she would be back later and headed out to her car. James went over to the window and yelled.

"C.J., where are you going?" Courtney did not respond to her husband. She was so angry at this point that she did not care where she went or when she was coming back. All she knew was that she needed to get away from him, and now. She got into her car and took off down the road. Her mind raced with thoughts of that house and what was happening to her relationship with her own husband.

Back home, James was having troubles of his own. He tried to call his wife and realized that she left her phone at home. He walked downstairs, told the kids that things would be okay, that mom was just upset.

"Is it about the dog?" Billy asked.

"No, why would it be about the dog?" James replied to his son's question.

"Penny barked the other day and mom came in and yelled at us until we told her it was two fifteen," Billy stated.

"Was that on Sunday?" James asked.

"Yup," Andy stated.

"Was it really two fifteen?" James asked.

"Yes, Daddy, it was and the dog was barking in the office," Billy replied.

"Okay, I believe you. Finish up your homework and then I want you guys to take turns getting in the shower and get ready for bed. Don't worry about mom. She will be home soon. She just needs time to cool off," James said and then headed toward the stairs.

James went into the office. He was looking for answers on his own. He pulled down the attic stairs and Penny began to bark. "It's okay, Penny, I am just going to check a few things out," he said. "I believe the boys. I should have believed my wife," he said and climbed the attic stairs.

James could not see anything. It was too dark. He reached over on the wall and pulled the cord for the light. He then walked a little bit further into the attic. He could see the furniture that Courtney had talked about and boxes of stuff everywhere. "Well, they left us quite a mess up here," he stated as he looked around. James went over to the box that Courtney had opened. He picked up a picture of the couple and wiped the dust off. He could see them sitting on a rock down by the creek. They looked very happy. James could not figure out why Courtney was told that he killed his wife and then himself.

Just as James was getting ready to open the next box, Penny began to bark. He did not pay any attention; he continued to pull at the tape on the box. This next box contained old papers including birth certificates and marriage licenses. He could barely make out the name on the first one. He believed it read Joseph P. Wells. The second one said Rebecca A. Wilcox. James folded up the marriage certificate and put it in his pocket. He really needed to support his wife so he wanted to show it to her. He then picked up the birth certificate. This one belonged to Joseph. It said that he was born right here at a hospital in Salem, N.Y. "He must have grown up here," James stated as he folded the certificate back up and put it in the box. James was just about to close the box when he felt a hand on his shoulder. He turned around and found no one there. He panicked, tripping over boxes on his way back to the ladder. He climbed down and shut the attic.

For the first time since this whole thing started, James felt what Courtney felt. He knew at this point that there was something going on in this house. Something in that attic did not want him there. He was now feeling bad for not believing his wife. James sat on his bed and began to cry. He was very angry with himself for not believing his wife, angry that she had been going through this all alone.

When James was able to pull himself together, he went to check on the boys. He could here that Billy was in the shower. He walked into Andy's room to find him sitting on his bed playing with Billy's Game Boy. "Hi Dad," Andy said as he got out of bed. "I was playing this game," he said and handed the game to his father.

"Cool," James said. "I really don't want to play it right now, but thanks for showing it to me," James said to his son, handing the game back to him.

"Is Mom coming home?" Andy asked his father.

"I am sure she will be home so," James replied.

What he was going to say was "soon," but he heard the front door close, and he knew that his wife was home. "See, mom is home now," James stated as Andy walked passed him and down the stairs.

By the time James got to the bottom of the stairs, Andy was hugging his mother. He could see that she had been crying, and he felt bad. He walked over to his wife and took the paper out of his pocket. "I believe you C.J. I am sorry," he said and handed the paper to his wife as Andy asked what it was.

"It is a paper for Mom, please go play so Mom and I can talk," James stated to his son.

"Alright Dad," Andy replied and headed off to play upstairs. James took Courtney by the hand and led her to the couch. "Please sit," he said and sat with her on the couch. Courtney sat next to her husband and just listened as he talked. "I talked to the boys about the dogs barking. I then went up to the attic. I looked at the pictures in the box you opened. Then I opened another box and found the certificate you are holding. C.J., I felt something, a hand, a hand on my shoulder. When I turned around, nothing was there. I believe you C.J., I believe you heard everything and saw everything. I want to help you to get these spirits out of our house," James stated and held Courtney's hand tight.

"James, I am so glad you finally believe me. I have been trying to tell you, but you did not get it," Courtney replied and hugged her husband. Finally, feeling relieved that she was not crazy, she smiled. She smiled for the first time in days, a smile that she had forgotten she had.

"Boys" James called as Courtney looked at him with a puzzling look. "Boys," he called again. She then looked at the certificate.

"Rebecca, that's his wife?" Courtney asked.

"Yeah," James replied and C.J. folded up the certificate and put it in her pocket for safe keeping.

"Coming," Andy replied as he ran down the stairs.

"What is it, Dad?" Billy said as he rounded the corner of the stairs.

"Well, Mom and I just wanted to let you know that we are alright. We are not arguing anymore," he said to his boys, holding Courtney's hand.

"Were you fighting about Linda?" Billy asked.

"Linda? No, this had nothing to do with that little girl. Anyways, get ready for bed. We will be right up to say goodnight."

Mr. and Mrs. Stealth walked up the stairs hand in hand, for the first time in weeks, they were in it together. They went into both boys rooms and said goodnight. Then they went into the bathroom and took a shower together. Courtney could not keep from kissing her husband. It occurred to her that they had not kissed in days. She could not remember the last time the two of them made love. She knew that would change tonight.

After they had showered, the couple headed into the bedroom, closing the door behind them. James gently took Courtney's towel off and began kissing her. He felt like it was their first time all over again. He has butterflies in his stomach and a school age grin on his face. He took Courtney by the hand and gently pulled her to the bed and made love to her.

With James and Courtney completely satisfied, Courtney opened the bedroom door. She could see the dog sitting and waiting for her. "Sorry girl, we just needed some time alone," Courtney stated and patted the dog on the head as she went to the bathroom to get a drink of water. She looked at the garbage can and remembered the lock of hair from Linda. "Linda, that is another story," she said. "James never said he understood her. Oh well, maybe he forgot about her with all this ghost shit happening," Courtney said and headed off to bed and held James tightly.

A few days later, the family was packing up to go to Grandmas for Billy's birthday. There had been no sign of weird behavior in the house, except Penny's barking. There was no movement in the attic or writing on the wall. It was as if the house was theirs, theirs and only theirs. Courtney, of course, did not believe that. She believed that they were just waiting for the right moment to appear again.

Courtney was putting the remaining bags in the car. She felt in her pocket to feel the lock of hair belonging to Linda. For some reason, she needed to have it with her. She felt as if Linda would want her to have it in the city. She felt Linda's attachment with this lock of hair. Courtney called the kids over to get in the car. James was locking the truck and closed the garage. He then locked the front door. For a second, just a second, he thought he saw a man standing inside the door. He looked again, but no one was there. He turned and headed to the car. "Should I tell C.J.? If I tell her, she will want to stay here," he said to himself and got into the car.

As the family backed out of the driveway, Courtney could feel someone watching them from inside the house. "James, James look!" she said as James stopped the car.

"What, C.J., look at what?" he replied and put the car in park.

"There, in the window, the living room window! Do you see him?" she said as she opened the car door.

"C.J. Wait!" James stated. But she was already on the porch staring in the window.

James and the boys got out of the car. "Mommy," Billy said "I saw a man in the window too! Who is he? Why is he in our house?" Billy asked.

"I think we should just go, C.J." James stated. "We need to get out of this house and regroup," he continued. "Come on boys. Let's get in the car," he said and gently took Courtney by the arm. "Hon let's go. We can take care of this when we get back," he said and the couple headed to the car. The entire time, Courtney was looking back over her shoulder. She really wanted to stay and discover more information about this house and the couple who previously lived there, but her son had a party to get to. So she really needed to go.

CHAPTER

NINE

THE SECOND PARTY

James, Courtney, Billy, Andy, and Penny arrived at Brenda's house late that night. The boys were exhausted and headed right to bed in the spare room. Courtney and James stayed up for a while talking to James' mother about the newly discovered spirits in their house. Brenda laughed, of course. She did not believe in ghosts. "You two are just making this up right? Trying to fool an old lady?" she laughed.

"I assure you, Mom, we are not teasing you. I swear to you I could feel his hand on my shoulder," James said. Then Courtney told his mother of how the previous owned killed his wife and then himself.

"I believe that the original owner of the home, Joseph Wells, killed his wife at two fifteen pm., because Penny always barks in the office of our house at that very time every day. She just walks in and sits down and barks, every day," Courtney told her mother-in-law.

"Well, I think you are both going crazy," she said and got up. "As far as this dog goes," she said as she reached down and pet Penny on the head. She is just getting used to the house and you are reading too much into the situation," she said and kissed her son on the cheek. "I am going to bed. See you in the morning," she continued and headed to bed.

It was a beautiful Saturday morning. The sun was shining and the birds were flying high in the sky. The family was just finishing up breakfast and getting ready to set up for Billy's party. Brenda was in the kitchen cooking pasta for her macaroni salad and potatoes for her potato salad. Courtney was blowing up balloons with the boys and James was setting up tables and chairs in the back yard. In the distance the phone rang. "I'll get it," Brenda said and wiped her hands on a towel and went in the other room to get the phone. "Courtney," she yelled. "It's for you." Courtney walked to the phone with a confused look on her face.

"Who would call me here?" she asked Brenda.

"I don't know. It sounds like a little girl to me," Brenda stated and handed the phone to Courtney.

"A little girl?" she questioned as she answered the phone. "Hello?"

"It's me Linda I want you to come home. They are being mean to me and I need you to come home," she said.

"Who is being mean to you and how did you get this number?" Courtney asked.

"THEY" are being mean to me and I need you to come home!" Linda demanded.

"I'm sorry, but I am not coming home until Sunday. Who gave you this number?" Courtney asked. Then she heard a scream on the other end of the phone, and Linda was gone.

"Linda?" Linda?' Courtney called, but she was gone.

Courtney looked at the caller I.D. She was surprised to see that the call came from her own house. "How the hell did she get in the house?" she yelled and headed out to where James was setting up for the party. "James! You are never going to believe what just happened. Linda called. She called from our house," she said and handed the phone to James. "Check the caller I.D. It is our number," she continued. "Your mom answered the phone and said it was a little girl calling and, sure enough, it was Linda. She wants me to come home. What do we do?" she asked.

James looked at the caller I.D. "Well, I guess we call the cops and have them check the house and make sure she is not there. If she is, they will make sure she is alright and ask her to leave. Then we will just go home after the party."

James called information and got the local sheriff for Salem. He reported that there was a possibility of someone calling from inside their house and the sheriff said he would send someone to check it out and give them a call back. James hung up the phone and told Courtney what the sheriff was going to do.

"I don't know, James, something is not right here," she said. How did she get in the house?" she continued. "How did she get your mom's number? That girl is so weird," she then stated.

"I don't know C.J," James stated.

"Well we locked up the house tight before we left, so how would she even get in the house?" he asked.

"I don't know I just don't know James. I think that we should go home tonight instead of staying until tomorrow," Courtney states.

"I agree. If someone got into our house, I want to get home to check and see how and to secure the house. Remember the man we thought we saw inside the house when we left? Who was that? Maybe he let her in." James replied.

"I don't know, James. All I know is that I want to go home and check on our house and see if Linda is alright."

"We will leave after the party," James replied.

A few hours later, the guests arrived. The party was a big hit. Billy had most of his friends from his old school there. Courtney and James got to see a few old friends as well. The boys were playing and having a blast. Brenda came out of the house with the cake and Billy had all his friends and family singing to him. He was a happy boy. Courtney was standing there watching with a smile on her face, but inside, she was waiting for a phone call from the sheriff's office. She wanted to know what was happening at her home. When the party ended and the guests were gone, Courtney began to pack up the car. She wanted to get on the road as soon as possible. "C.J.," she heard James calling her.

Courtney turned to see James coming out the front door with the phone in his hand. He approached his wife. "That was the sheriff. He went to the house but there was no one there," he stated.

"Well, we both know that she was there," she replied.

The sheriff said there was no sign of anyone being there. He said she could have come and been gone before he got there. Then he asked her name and all I could tell him was that her name was Linda. He wanted a last name. I did tell him that she lived on the road somewhere in the neighborhood," James stated. "Get this Court, they have no information of anyone else on our dirt road who has children," he continued. "Are you sure that she lives on our road?" he asked. Courtney was shocked. She could not understand what he was asking.

"Of course I am sure," she stated. "She said that she lived a few houses down the road. I don't think she goes to school. It appears that her parents don't take care for her well. I think that they are just loners," she continued. "I don't know James, but there is something about that girl and her family," she stated and went back to packing the bags into the car.

"I know C.J., I agree. We really do need to get home. I think that I would feel better getting home and checking the house," James said and helped his wife get the car ready to go.

With the car all packed, they said goodbye to Brenda. "I am going to miss you so much," she said hugging both of her grand kids. Then she went over to her son and gave him a hug and a kiss. "I wish you would just stay here, or just move back home. If there are things happening at the house, you should not be there," she stated.

"Mom, we will be fine. We are going to get to the bottom of this and take care of it. That is our home and we are not staying here," James said very sternly. Then he went and got into the car and started it up. The last one to say goodbye was Courtney. She hugged her mother-in-law and got into the car. Then James put the car in drive and headed home.

CHAPTER

TEN

"THEY" RETURN

The family arrived home late on Saturday night. Courtney woke her boys up as they entered the driveway. She was the first one out of the car. She went on the porch and opened the front door for James with the boy's right behind him. She told the boys to head right up to bed as she unlocked the front door. Courtney entered the house to feel a cold breeze hit her in the face. "James, why is it so cold in here?" she asked. It was so cold that Courtney could see her breath in front of her. Then, all of a sudden, it began to feel warm again. "James," she said. "Did you feel that?"

"Yeah, I felt it. Boys, wait right here while I check the house. I don't want you going upstairs yet. Penny, come," he said, bringing the dog with him. James checked the boy's rooms and the toy room. They were all clear. He then went into the master bedroom. He could feel a cold draft. He was not sure what it was, but he needed to find out. He walked further into the room, holding Penny's collar. He entered the office area to see that the drop stairs to the attic were down. "What the hell?" he said out loud to himself. "I know that they were up when we left," he said as he started to climb the stairs.

James stood in the attic. He turned on the light, looked around and found nothing out of place. He walked further into the attic to have a better look. All that James could see was the open window. "So, that is how she got in here," he said. Then James closed the window and headed back down the attic stairs. He walked out of the bedroom and to the living room where the family was. "Okay, boys, you can head to bed." Andy looked at Billy and then at his mother. "Mommy, are sure that it is safe?"

"Daddy said it was fine, hon, you will be alright," C.J. replied.

"I would not let you back in this house if there were something wrong boys," James added and pointed to the stairs. "Now go to bed guys. Everything is fine."

Courtney and James watched as the boys headed to bed. Then James turned to Courtney, "Well C.J. I figured out how Linda got in here. She must have used a ladder and climbed in the attic window because the drop stairway to the attic were down. I closed the window so we should be alright now," he continued.

"How on earth did that little girl get a ladder that long up to the attic? She had to have help, James," Courtney stated and sat on the couch.

"I really don't know if it was even her. All I know is the house looks alright and I don't think anything is missing," he stated. "So, unless you are scared and want to leave the house, I am going to go unload the car and I am going to bed." he added.

"I don't want to leave. The boys are in bed and everything seems fine. I'll help," Courtney replied.

"No, I can do it," he stated and kissed his wife. Courtney had to help. She needed to get the lock of Linda's hair out of her suitcase. She could not sleep knowing it was not in the house. For some reason, she needed Linda's hair near her at all times.

Courtney followed James outside to get the luggage. She grabbed the suitcase that had her belongings in it and another one that held the bathroom supplies. "I told you that I could get it," James stated as he grabbed a few things from the trunk of the car.

"I know, but I wanted to help," she replied as she headed to the house. She carried the suitcases up the stairs and set the small suitcase in the bathroom and continued to her room. She quickly opened up the suitcase and took out the lock of hair. She gently placed it in her nightstand before James could see it. She then zipped the suitcase back up and set it on the floor next to the bed.

James entered the bedroom to see that Courtney was sitting on the bed with Penny, watching the late night news. "I am so tired," James said as he took off his shirt.

"Me, too," Courtney replied. "James, I am so glad we came home early. Who knows who could have gotten in here if Linda had left the door open? We could have come home to find our house was robbed."

"I know I am glad we came home too." James stated climbing into bed. Courtney and James awoke the next morning to a voice in the hallway. "James, James, who is that?" Courtney asked, as she got out of bed.

"I am not sure, but I am going to find out," he stated as he got out of bed. The two walked to the bedroom door. James held Courtney behind him to protect her. He entered the hallway to find no one was there. He looked in the boy's rooms and the toy room and found no one. "I recognize that voice," Courtney said. "It is the same voice I heard the other day telling me to get out."

"What is he saying?" James asked his wife as they checked the bathroom.

"I don't know. I can't make it out. It sounds like he is talking to someone else in the distance. Like we are hearing one side of a conversation," Courtney replied. Then they heard another response. This response was clear as day. It was a woman's voice. She was screaming "NO, PLEASE, NO," The couple heard a gunshot and a thud on the office floor.

"James, what is happening?" Courtney asked and began to cry. "I don't know, but I am going to find out!" he yelled and ran to the office.

"James!" Courtney yelled trying to stop him, but James was already in the office by the time she got her words out.

James entered the office to find a blood splattered wall and blood spattered computer desk. He looked around but there was no one there. "What the hell?" he questioned. "C.J, come see this," he called out to his wife. Courtney rounded to corner to the office wall to see James calling her. To her surprise, she saw blood.

"James, whose blood is this, Where is Penny?" Is it hers?" she stated in a panic.

"No, I think it was from the woman screaming, but where is she?" he responded as he began to look around the bedroom.

"James, this house is trying to tell us something. I want to get the boys out of here!" she yelled.

"I think you are right, I think the couple who died here is trying to tell us something," he responded. "But I don't think they are going to hurt the boys. I think they are upset that we are here," he said as he grabbed a towel out of the hamper in the corner of the bedroom. "Now help me clean this mess up please," he said. Just as he was about to wipe the blood from the desk, every bit of the blood vanished. Courtney watched as her husband's face turned pale. He was in shock at what was happening to them. "Courtney I don't get it. What the hell is happening?"

"I am not sure, James," she responded and went to her husband's side. "Come on, hon let's get out of here. I will make you some coffee," she said and looked at the clock. "It is almost six o'clock so we can sit downstairs and talk. Maybe we can come up with an idea on how to get these, well I guess we have to say it, "ghosts" out of our house," she said. "Okay, I will be right down. I want to check on the boys first."

Courtney went downstairs and started the coffee. Then her husband joined her in the kitchen. "Are the kids alright?" she asked.

"Yes, they are fine," James replied. and sat down at the table.

"I think we need to get back into the attic, James. I think when I went up there for the first time it started a chain reaction in this house. I think we may find answers up there," Courtney said.

"I agree with you C.J. We can go up there once the boys are awake and playing. I would hate to wake them up after our long trip this weekend," he said.

"I agree," Courtney replied as she handed her husband a cup of coffee.

"Thanks, Hon," James replied.

CHAPTER

ELEVEN

THE FINDING

With the boys playing outside, the couple headed up the stairs. "James, what if we really stir something up in the attic? Then what? We don't know what we are doing when it comes to ghosts," Courtney said and grabbed her husband's hand as they got to the top step.

"Well, we will just figure out what we need to do," he replied and continued to walk toward the office. As he rounded the corner, he could see Penny sleeping on the spare bed. He walked in and grabbed the pull string to the attic. Courtney reached out and grabbed his hand.

"James, are you sure, really sure that we should do this? I know I said we should before, but I am so scared," Courtney stated.

"Courtney," he said and removed her hand from his. "We have to take back this house and this is how," he said and pulled the stairs to the attic down.

James and Courtney ascended the stairs and entered the attic. As soon as James turned the light switch on, the bulb blew out. "Well, that figures," he said and continued into the attic with Courtney right behind him. Just as James was about to pick up a picture, he could hear a giggle, a giggle of a little girl. "Did you hear that C.J.?" he questioned.

"Yeah, I heard it, James," she said.

"Can we go now?" she asked.

"No, we have to find out how to take our house back," James said and looked at the picture in his hand.

"Court, come see this girl," he said. "Maybe she was their daughter or something," James continued. Courtney came over and took the picture. She looked at it for just a second.

"This is Linda!" she exclaimed. "James this is the girl from down the road but look it can't be. This picture looks like it is very old. How is this possible?" Courtney said to her husband, handing him the picture. "Look James, and if you don't believe me, ask the boys. She is wearing the same dress that she wore when I saw her, only it is not ripped or dirty. Do you think?" Courtney began. "Do you think that she is dead?" she finished.

"Well C.J., it sure looks that way," James said.

Courtney reached into her pocket, feeling for the lock of hair that she had of Linda. She remembered at once that she laid it in her nightstand drawer.

"James, I have a lock of hair that I found of hers the day of Billy's party. She is real. How could I have her hair if she is dead?" she said.

"What do you mean you have her hair?" he asked as he put down the picture and headed over to his wife. "C.J., what are you talking about?"

"I am talking about the day we had Billy's party. She was here, in this house and when I would not play with her she left. I asked you if you saw her and you left without going out to the party, but her hair was in the bathroom and I took it. I don't even know why, but I had to have it," she said.

"Courtney, why do you think you had to have her hair? You are making no sense at all," James stated and looked deep into his wife's eyes, trying to figure out what she was thinking.

"I, I don't really know. I just needed to have a part of her close to me. James, she needed me from the first day I saw her and maybe, just maybe, she was trying to tell me all along that she was, well that she was a ghost," Courtney responded.

"Maybe, but how is she related to the couple in this house? How is she related to Joseph and Rebecca Wells? And what happened to her?" James asked and then answered his own question. "I am not sure, but we are figuring this out. I am not leaving this attic until we get some truth about this couple and this little girl, C.J." Courtney was so glad that she had finally told her husband about the lock of hair. She wrapped her arms about him and sobbed.

"James, I thought that I was going crazy, I am so glad that you are here for me and we are in this together," she said and looked up at her husband. "I love you," she added.

The two of them began looking around the attic for documents about the past. They uncovered the furniture that was there since the early sixties and began wiping the dust off the old photos. They were staring face to face with the past, the past life of this house. "James, why would all this stuff be left behind?" Courtney asked.

"I don't know. I just don't know," he replied and finished cutting open the box he was working on. James looked into the box to see an old photo of Linda with a couple who looked like they may have been in their thirties. It was a photo that definitely looked like a photo from the sixties. This photo was absolute proof that C.J. has seen a ghost and that Linda, Linda herself, must have died as a child. "Court, come see this," he said to his wife who was still dusting off some of the furniture.

Courtney walked over to where her husband was standing. "What is it, James?" she asked.

"It's a photo; take a look at it," he stated and handed the picture to his wife.

Courtney took the photo. "That's Linda again. Who are those people with her, I wonder?" she asked.

"Well let's take the picture out of the frame and see if it is labeled," James stated.

"Okay, well let's take it downstairs and do it so we can check on the boys," Courtney replied.

"Alright," James said.

Courtney was wiping off the picture when she looked up and saw him. He was standing behind James, just looking at her. She could see he was trying to tell Courtney something, but she could not hear anything. "James, James turn around slowly and see if you see what I see," Courtney stated standing very still. James turned to see Joseph P. Wells looking at him. He was talking, but Courtney and James could not hear what he was saying.

"Courtney, get out of the attic. I am coming right behind you," James stated very calmly. He was not sure what this ghost wanted, but the look on his face was telling him that he wanted James out of his attic. Joseph was saying something and staring at James. His eyes were fixated on James' eyes. James slowly descended the stairs with his eyes locked on the spirit of Joseph Wells. He waited for Courtney to get out of the way so he could close the stairs. He could hear the dog barking. James looked at his watch and sure enough it was two fifteen pm. "That is why this dog acts strangely at this time, C.J. I bet that Joseph shows up every day at this time in this attic," he stated and went over to pet Penny on the head. This is beginning to make sense. He shows up every day at this time because something important happened at this time of the day for him," James stated.

"I don't care what happened to him, I want him out of our house, James," Courtney replied heading to the window to check on the kids.

"I do too. Let's get the boys a snack and check out this picture a bit better more closely," James stated and went out the bedroom door.

Courtney and James were sitting at the dining room table with the boys, eating cookies and drinking milk. James turned over the picture and began to take the back off of the picture. "What picture is that, Dad?" Andy asked.

"It is a picture of a little girl and what I think is her family. Mom and I found it up in the attic and we wanted to check it for a date to see how old it is," James replied. The boys finished their snack and took off outside to play, leaving James and Courtney to tend to the picture.

James had the picture out of the frame. He turned it over and could barely make out a few names on the back. "I think this says Bart, Linda, and Mary Kelly, but I am not sure about the name Mary," he said and handed the picture to his wife. "What do you think it says?" Courtney took the picture and read the names.

"You are correct. This is the Kelly family. James, Linda is really dead. She was here in this house, she played with our kids. How is that possible? How does a dead child play with children?" she asked.

"I don't know C.J. All I know is that I want to get this man out of our house and find out how he is connected to Linda," he replied. "I think we better get more answers," he said. "The only way to get the answers we need is to get back in the attic."

Courtney and James headed back to the attic. This time Courtney went up first and James followed her. The two of them began sifting through boxes of pictures, looking for answers. "James, I found another picture of Linda. She is down by the water in this one," she said and walked over and handed him the picture. "This looks like the shore behind the house, C.J." he said.

"I know. I have played in that very same spot with the kids. James, I saw her down there one day when the boys were swimming," she replied.

Just as James was about to put the picture aside and continue looking around, the picture actually changes. "C.J., check this out," he said and showed his wife the picture. The two of them stood still and watched as the little girl in the picture walked into one of the caves by the water. She then turned to the front of the cave and stopped, almost as if she were looking right at us. "Over there," she said and pointed to the back of the cave where there was a pile of rocks. "Dig, please dig! Over there! I don't want to play with them anymore!" she yelled and then the picture when right back to the original picture.

"What the hell was that? Did you see that C.J? Did she just talk to us?" James asked as he dropped the picture to the floor and broke the glass.

"James, she is trying to tell us something," Courtney said as she picked up the shattered pieces of glass and the picture frame.

"I see that. She wants us to dig in one of the caves; but why?" James stated as he grabbed one of the empty boxes for Courtney to put the broken glass in.

"I don't know, but I sure as hell am going to dig in that cave tomorrow when the boys are in school," Courtney replied.

"Well, I am digging too. I will take the day off and help," James responded. "I am not letting you do this alone."

"Let's keep looking around. Maybe we can get her to tell us more," Courtney stated.,

James and Courtney spent most of the afternoon searching for old pictures and uncovering all the furniture. They swept up most of the dust, dirt and cob webs. This whole time, nothing happened. No pictures that talked and no images of the dead.

Courtney decided that she needed to get dinner started and James figured he would come downstairs as well. Neither one of them had spent any real time with the boys. James wanted to have some fun with them. Courtney went into the kitchen and took out the chicken to put on the grill. She then chopped up the vegetables for a salad, put some broccoli in the microwave and took the tray of chicken out to the porch to grill. She watched as James and the boys were playing ball. She laughed a bit, because playing a game with three people can be challenging.

With the chicken grilling, she went back in the house and set the table. She put the salad and dressing on the table and grabbed the broccoli out of the microwave, brought that to the table as well. She then went out and flipped the chicken and waited for it to cook. She watched the boys playing in the yard and they were laughing with their father. With the chicken finished, Courtney turned off the grill and carried the platter back to the front door and headed into the house. As Courtney walked into the dining area, she dropped the plate on the floor. "James!" she screamed. "James!" she screamed again as she headed back to the front door. "James!" she yelled one more time to get his attention. As she did, James came running with the boy's right behind him.

"What is it, C.J.?" he asked.

"Boys, go play for a minute, I need to talk to Daddy," she said to the kids and then took James by the hand and led him in the house. "You have to see this," she stated.

James walked into the house to see words written on the wall of the dining room in crimson blood. The words read HIDDEN SHADDOW. My name is Linda. HELP ME! "Okay, I think she is definitely trying to get us to help her now," James stated."But how Linda?" James questioned as he looked up at the ceiling. "How do we help you? Just as James was about to speak again, the words appeared. FIND JOSEPH. "Okay, how do we find him Linda? Where is he?" James asked and watched as all the words disappeared from the wall.

"James, what does she mean by "FIND JOSEPH? I thought

Joseph was the ghost from the attic?"

"He is C.J. I think she wants us to find his body. Maybe that is how she will be set free. I think he did something to her," James stated, and walked over and hugged his wife. "Don't worry, we will find his body or whatever she wants us to do. In the meantime, we need to clean up this mess from the chicken and order dinner for the boys and act like everything is fine until they go to bed. We don't want to upset or scare them," James said as he began to pick up the platter off the floor and put the chicken on it. Courtney went to the phone to order pizza then got the mop out to clean the floor.

With the boys fed, showered, and in bed for the night, C.J. and James sat on the couch and talked about the weekend events. They needed to get back in that attic to get more answers and they needed Linda's help in finding what she wanted them to do. They also talked about going to the cave that they saw in the picture that morning. James turned on the television. He wanted to catch the weather for tomorrow to make sure it was a good day to go to the creek. He could see the weather man talking about clouds moving in the afternoon. Then a familiar face appeared on the screen, a face that Courtney and James both recognized, but could not place at first. This woman began to speak. "It began in the nursery. I was unaware of his actions, and then I found out about the rape. I tried to stop him, but he killed her and buried her," then the woman was gone and the program snapped back to the normal weather reporter.

"Did you see and hear that, C.J.?" James asked.

"Yes, that was Rebecca, Joseph's wife," she said as she got up and went to get the picture they had found the other day. "Here, James," she said and gave him the picture.

"It's her, isn't it?' she asked and sat back down next to her husband.

"Yeah, it's her. Did she say rape? I hope to God she was not talking about Linda," James stated and looked at his wife.

"If so, that explains why she wants us to help her. I think he killed her," James stated.

"I bet that is why he killed his wife. She found out about Linda and he could not let Rebecca tell," Courtney stated to her husband. "James, what are we going to do? We have to help set Linda free from this house and the hell she has been living in."

"We are going to the creek tomorrow and we are getting back in that attic as well. Did she say the nursery, our office?" James asked.

"Yes, that is what she said. Maybe that is where it happened. That explains the dog's behavior," he said and took C.J. by the hand.

"Come on hon, let's try to get some sleep," he said.

"I can't sleep James. I want to help Linda," she replied. "Well, we can't help her tonight. It's late and we have to get up with the boys. How about a hot bath?" James asked.

"Alright, maybe that will help."

James drew his wife a bath. He helped her get in the tub and dribbled in her bubble bath. He then went and poured her a glass of wine and took it to her.

"I am going to check my e-mail and then I will be back to sit with you until you're finished," he said and handed his wife the glass of wine and kissed her on the forehead. "I love you," he whispered and then turned and headed out the door to the office.

James was sitting at the desk in the office checking his e-mail. He was returning mail from his mother. She was asking how things were after they had gotten home last night and if they figured out why the call they received came from inside the house. James, of course, was lying to his mom. He told her that everything was fine. That Linda just came over to see if Courtney was home and then called. No big deal, he told her. She was just a lonely little girl in the neighborhood. He could not tell her the truth about the ghosts. If he did, Mom would demand that they leave that house or say that James and Courtney were crazy. So, he told her what she wanted to hear.

He was just in the middle of shutting down the computer when he could see Joseph in the computer monitor. It was as if he was standing right behind him. He turned to look, but he was not there. James shut off the computer and left the office, calling Penny to come with him. He let the dog out and checked the yard while Penny relieved herself. He looked toward the path that lead toward the creek. He wanted so badly to go down the caves right now but it was dark and he needed to wait until he could see better. Then he turned, called the dog and headed back into the house, locking the door behind him. He headed back upstairs to where Courtney was.

James opened the bathroom door to find Courtney sitting on the floor with her robe on, crying. "C.J., what is it?" James asked as he knelt down next to his wife and put his arm around her.

"I just want our house back. We moved here to give our kids a better life and this is what we get?" Courtney cried.

"I know, C.J.," he said and helped her to her feet. "We will get our house back. We just have to figure out how; that's all," he continued. "I think that Linda will help us."

"I know," Courtney replied as the two of them headed off to the bedroom.

Courtney and James climbed into bed and cuddled up next to

each other. Neither of them could sleep so they turned the television on and watched for a while. Eventually, they closed their eyes and drifted off for the night, both holding each other tightly.

On Monday morning, James woke early. He called the office and talked to the foreman on the job, informing him that he was in charge, for the day. He could hear Courtney getting the boys up for school. Then he let the dog out and started breakfast. When the family was finished with breakfast, James and Courtney took the boys to the bus stop. They said goodbye to the boys and then headed back to the house, parked the car and went inside.

Courtney was the first one in the house. "James," she called. "Are we going down to the caves now?" she asked as she held the door open for her husband.

"Just as soon as we get dressed," he replied as he headed toward the stairs.

"Okay, I will be right up to get dressed as soon as I put fresh water down for the dog," Courtney replied. She watched for a second as Penny took a drink. Then she headed upstairs, passing James on his way down. "I will be ready in just a second. I need to put on jeans and I will be right down," she said as she hustled up the stairs to change.

Courtney entered the bedroom and went to the night stand. "If I am going into the cave to see what I think I am going to see, I want to take her hair with me," she said, and then threw on a pair of jeans from her drawer. She tucked the lock of Linda's hair into her back pocket and went down stairs. She could see that James was sitting on the couch, watching the news, waiting for her. "Just got to throw on my sneakers, and I am ready," she stated.

"Okay," James replied and got up off the couch and waited by the door for Courtney.

With Courtney ready, she grabbed two flashlights out of the closet. She called Penny and hooked her up to her leash, and headed out the door with James right behind her. James closed the door, took one of the flashlights and took Courtney by the hand. "Let's go," he said and the couple headed out to the yard to get on the trail to the creek. They were unsure of what they were going to find, but they both knew that they were going to find it together.

Penny was leading the way down the trail. She was sniffing everything she could along the way. She had not been on this trail yet and she was excited to take in all the smells of nature. She led the couple to the end of the path, stopping right at the edge of the water. "Okay, now what?" James asked. "How do we cross the creek?" he questioned.

"Well, I am sure if we follow the path, we can find a way across," Courtney responded as she began walking down the edge of the creek.

"Are you coming, James?" she asked.

"Yeah, I'm coming. I was just looking to see if we could cross here, but we can't," he said and followed his wife until he caught up with her and Penny.

The couple walked for about a quarter of a mile until they came to an old bridge, a bridge that looked like it had not been used it years. It was an old foot bridge that had a few planks missing. "Well, I guess this is the way across to the cave," Courtney said looking at James. "Do you think we can make it?"

"I think we will be okay," James stated as he stepped on the first plank to test it out. "Besides, the worst thing that will happen is that we get wet," he said with a smile on his face.

"True," Courtney replied. "Come, Penny," she said and let

Penny lead the way across the creek.

Penny, Courtney, and James were now on the other side of the creek headed back to the opening of the caves. A chill ran down Courtney's spine. She could feel that someone or something was watching them. She was unsure, but her fear was confirmed when she felt Penny pull on the leash and start to bark. She was headed in the direction of one of the caves. James reached over and grabbed Penny's leash to help control her. Penny had never given Courtney a problem before, but something was getting her attention. James and Courtney were sure that it was not something they wanted to deal with.

"Heal, Penny!" James demanded and Penny snapped out of her trance and sat at James' feet.

"James, are you sure we should keep going?" Courtney asked.

"Well, we will never find out what we need to if we don't continue, C.J," James replied.

"I know, but if Penny is acting like this, maybe we don't want to know what is in the cave she is barking at," Courtney replied.

"Well, if you want to find Linda or whatever is in this cave, we need to go forward," James replied and started walking with Penny by his side.

"You are right; I am just not sure what is in that cave and I want to make sure that we are safe, that's all," she said. She could feel, with every step closer to the cave, the feeling of something evil. She could not pin point it, but she was scared for herself and her husband. She knew that they needed to do this, but she did not have to like it, and she didn't.

James and Penny were the first at the cave opening. They stood there and waited for Courtney to catch up. James could barely see inside. He could only make out a cavern in the opening. As Courtney approached, he turned on the flashlight. "Are you ready?" he asked.

"I think so," she responded and turned on her flash light.

James took a deep breath and took a step inside the cave with his wife right by his side. Penny was pulling at the leash and barking toward the back of the cavern. "James, I think she is trying to tell us something. Maybe we should let her lead the way," Courtney stated.

"I agree," replied James as Penny led them deeper into the cave to the next opening. She then began to sniff the ground and took off, pulling James deeper and deeper into the cave with Courtney chasing after them. "What is it, girl? What do you smell?" James questioned, already knowing what was happening. Both Courtney and James knew what they were going to find in that cave. They knew from the second they set out on this trip what they were going to find, but they just never talked about it until now.

"James," she began. Penny is going to find her, isn't she?" she asked.

"We both know that she will, C.J., but we have to let her do it," he continued. "That is the only way we can help set her

free."

"I know, but I wish to God she was alive, or at least died a better way than this," Courtney stated.

"Me too," James replied.

The couple followed Penny to the corner of one of the caverns to a pile of rocks. These rocks looked like they had not been moved in years. Courtney felt a chill down her spine, the same chill she had felt before. "James, it is her, under the rocks. Her body is there. I just know it."

"Well, it is safe to say that we don't know," he said. "Never mind, I am not going to try to sugar coat this. It is her. We both know it," James replied as the couple started to move the rocks.

James had moved about a dozen rocks out of the way when he came across the first bones. The bones looked like bones of a foot. Courtney let out a scream and dropped the rock she was carrying and grabbed her husband by the shirt. "James, we need to call the police!" Courtney yelled.

"I know Courtney, let's get outside the cave so I can get reception," he replied as they walked to the entrance of the cave, leaving Penny sitting by the bones they found.

James picked up his phone and walked the path, with Courtney waiting at the entrance of the cave. He walked for a few seconds until he had reception, and then dialed 911. "911, what is your emergency?" the dispatcher asked.

"My name is James Stealth. My wife and I found some bones in a cave down by the creek behind our house. They are human bones we believe," he stated.

"Are you sure they are human?" the dispatcher asked. "There are a lot of animals that can get lost in the woods and it could be an animal."

"Well, it looks very human to me. I think it is a foot. It has all the little toe bones or whatever they are called," James said.

"Okay, I will send the police right away. Can someone show them where they are going?" she asked.

"I will have my wife meet them at the trail by our house. It is the first house on the left on Beacon. Do you know where that is?"

"I sure do sir. They should be there shortly." James hung up the phone and went back to where his wife was standing.

"Court, can you go back to the beginning of the trail and wait for the cops? They are going to come to the house and you can show them how to get here."

"Sure," she stated. "Keep an eye out for Penny in case she comes out of the cave," she said.

"I will, but I am sure that she is not going to leave that body until she has to," James replied and watched as his wife took off down the foot bridge.

The police arrived with a coroner's truck behind them. They all approached Courtney, who was now walking toward them. "Hi, my name is Courtney," she said as she put her hand out to shake hands with the officer and the coroner.

"I am officer McCabe, and this is the coroner Pat Hosner. We are waiting for a few investigators to show up. Then we will follow you to the cave where you believe you found human remains," the officer stated.

They waited for just a few minutes as Courtney told the story of finding the bones in the cave. She explained that and only that. She kept to herself the fact that she was haunted by a ghost and she knew in her heart who the bones belonged to. She did not want them to think she was crazy, so she figured she would let them do their job, and hope they figured out who she was.

Within a half hour, the whole team of police, investigators, and the coroner were at the cave. They had James go in and get the dog out, and taped off the cave with crime scene tape. James and

Courtney watched from a distance as the officers began bringing out the bones. They had bags and bags, labeled with red zipped tops. There were about six investigators with cameras. Courtney was sure they were taking pictures of the bones. It was quite a sight to see. All these men working hard at trying to make sure that they had everything they needed to take care of the case at hand.

Office McCabe approached James and Courtney. He needed to get information about what time they found the bones, about the bones that they had found, and if they moved any. He walked up to James, bent down, took off his rubber gloves and pet Penny on her head. "So let me make sure I got this right. You went in the cave, and just moved the rocks around? Can I ask why?" James did not miss a beat.

"Well, the dog took off and ran into the corner barking. She ran over to the rock pile and she was pawing them and barking. We moved the rocks to see what she was barking at. That is when we found the bones and we called 911," he said.

"Okay, so no one moved any of the remains then?" he asked as he was taking notes.

"No, we left them right where we found them and left the cave," James replied.

"Thanks for the information. You guys are free to go," he stated and thanked them for calling it in.

James looked at his watch. "Shit, C.J., we have to go, it is almost two and the boys will be getting home soon," he said.

"Alright, I wish we could stay, but we do need to get back for the boys," Courtney replied and the two of them headed back to the path. "James, how are we going to tell the kids about this? You know we have to. It will make the news and kids at school will be talking about it," she stated.

"Well, we just tell them what we know, that we found bones; they will find out the rest in time. I think that is the best way to handle it," James stated.

"Okay, if that is what you think is best, I agree with you," Courtney replied.

Courtney and James walked to the bus stop and met the boys. They explained that they took a walk to the caves and told them the same story they told the police officers. Billy, being so inquisitive, asked how many people would be coming to the house about their investigation and if his Mom and Dad were going to be on the news.

"I don't know, I guess I never thought about making it on the news," James said, looking at Courtney for input.

"We will just have to wait and see what is going to happen. I am sure that we will at least here from the police about the case," Courtney added.

Back at the house, the boys were looking at all the official vehicles that came to the house. They were looking at the equipment in the police car. Then they went to the window of a hummer that was sitting next to the cop car. They were trying to get a glimpse of what the police had inside. They then went over to the coroner's truck. Andy wanted no part of it. He stood back and waited for Billy to finish looking around. "Let's go boys. We don't need to be all over the vehicles," James stated. "Let's go in the house and try to find something to keep busy while they do their work at the cave," he said and waved the boys to come toward the house.

Billy, being the inquisitive little boy that he is, stood in the living room staring out the window. He wanted to see everything that the police were bringing out of the cave. He watched as the cops loaded bags into the back of the police car and watched as the crime scene investigator noted everything that they had found. He could see that one of the officers was headed toward the front door. "Mom!" he yelled. "A cop is coming to the front door," he said, as he ran over to open it.

Billy opened the door and stood face to face with Officer McCabe. He wanted so badly to ask him questions about what he found, but his mom stopped him and told him to go upstairs, that this was something he did not need to get involved in. Billy tried to argue, but it was no use. His father was coming to the door and he knew that his battle to stay and talk to the officer was lost. He stomped his feet as he slowly walked to the stairs.

"Sorry officer," Courtney began. "You know how kids can be. Come on in," she continued.

"It's fine, I have kids of my own," he replied and walked in the front door. He took a pad of paper out of his shirt pocket and opened it. He clicked his pen and began. "Okay, so it was you and your husband James, no one else, right?' he asked.

"Right, just us and the dog," Courtney replied.

"You were just out for a walk and then went in the cave?" he asked

"Yes," Courtney replied.

"And I know I asked you this before, but you didn't touch any of the remains, right?"

"Correct," Courtney replied. As the officer continued to talk, James came back down the stairs from taking care of Billy.

"Hello, officer," he stated and shook his hand.

"Hi, I was just finishing up my investigation. I thank you both for reporting your findings," he stated and walked out the front door. By this time, all the other vehicles were gone. The only thing left was a trace of tire tracks and a bit of trampled grass.

Later that evening, the family settled in to watch a movie. James could hear people talking outside the house. He got up, went to the window and called Courtney. "C.J., you have to see this," he said waving for her to come to the window. Courtney got up with both boys right at her side. They went to the window and could see a news truck parked in front of their house. "Well, it looks like we made it to the news. Also looks like our house is going to be on television," James stated. Billy and Andy both rushed to the front door to go out and get in front of the camera. "I don't think so!" James yelled. "Back away from that door," he demanded. Both of the kids backed off and just watched out the window. Courtney went to the phone. "James we have to call our parents. We don't want them to hear this on the news," she said as she began to dial her mother's number. "Hi Mom," she began. She then told her the story of how they found human remains in the cave behind their house. She was careful not to tell her too much about what she believed, that it was Linda, a ghost that has been haunting their house. Her mother was very concerned for how the boys were dealing with the news. "Mom, the boys are fine. They actually think it is cool that we are going to be on the news, well, at least the house is anyway." Just as Courtney spoke, a reporter was walking to the front door. "Shit! Mom, I have to go. Reporters are at the front door. I will call you back."

James and Courtney stood by the door with the boys. They were waiting for the knock and they didn't know what to do. "James, do we really want to talk to them?" Courtney asked.

"I don't know." I am not sure that it will be a good idea," he said and then there came the knock. The couple had to think of what they wanted to do, and fast.

"James, whatever you want to do, I am fine with it." James took a deep breath and opened the front door.

"Hi, are you James Stealth?" the reporter asked.

"Yes, yes I am," James replied.

"Well, my name is Brad," the reporter said and put out his hand. With no response from James, he withdrew his unwelcome hand shake then continued. "I am here to talk to you about the remains that were found by the creek. May I come in?"

James looked at Courtney. "I don't think we should talk to a reporter until the police finish their investigation," James said.

"Okay, well, can we at least go through your lawn to get down to the creek? Can you tell me what cave the remains were found in?" the reporter asked.

"Well Sir, the answer to both of your questions is no. I will not help you get information until the police say I can. Now please leave."

"We are just trying to," he began, but James shut the door in the reporters face. "That ought to shut him up! I can't believe that I told him I could not help him and he still tried to talk his way into getting information," he said looking out the window making sure they were leaving. He watched as the reporter stood at the edge of their property, being filmed as he was talking about today's events. He could see the reporter pointing toward the trail to the creek and the caves. He then watched as he loaded his equipment into the truck and he and his camera crew drove away. James then turned and spoke to Courtney. "Well, looks like our names will definitely be on the news."

"I better call my mom back, James, and you need to call your mom too. They will worry if we don't," Courtney said.

When the calls were made, and the house had settled down for the night, Courtney had one question she needed answered. "James, are we ever going tell them that we have seen her ghost? Are we going to tell the truth?" she then asked.

"C.J., people will think we are crazy if we tell them. I think we are better off trying to see if the story ends here now that her bones have been found,"he replied.

"I don't think it is over. I am sure that we still have to find Joseph. I am not sure where he is buried, but I am surely going to find out," Courtney stated.

Courtney and James went upstairs to bed. They turned on the news to see what the reporter had to say. They waited for the weather to be announced, and then listened as the reporter began to tell their tale.

"Human remains were found today, the remains of what the police believe, by the size of the bones, are a child. They were found down at some old cave behind the old Wells' estate. The estate lay empty for years, until just a few months ago when the Stealth family purchased the land. It was this family that made the discovery in the cave. I have talked to the officer in charge. He is unable to identify the remains at this time. All he was able to tell me was that they were going to try to identify the bones by dental records and right now they are running tests on the remains."

With the story over, James told Courtney that they should try to get some sleep. It would be back to school for the boys tomorrow, but as for James, he was taking the week off to help his wife uncover what was happening in that house. He would be available for further investigation by the police and keep anyone other than the cops off his property. No one was going to have access to that cave unless they found another way in. "In the morning, I will put a fence by the entrance to the trail for the creek. I think I will also purchase an alarm system.

"I think that is a good idea. If someone gets hurt, it would be our responsibility. We own the property right to the edge of the water, so, if someone falls in, we are in deep shit," Courtney replied. "Now let's try to get to sleep. We have to get up with the boys and I am sure that people will be inquisitive and will try to get down to the creek tomorrow," she said and kissed her husband, and they tried to sleep.

Billy was the first one awake. He was downstairs getting his cereal when his dad came down. "Morning, Dad," he stated as he gave his father a hug.

"Good morning. You are up early," James said.

"I know. I couldn't sleep. I can't wait to go to school and tell all my friends about the bones and about the coroner being here with the investigators and reporters," Billy stated.

"Okay, slow down, this is not a fun thing. Someone died," he said.

"I know Dad, but if it is bones, they died a while ago and I just think that talking about it with my friends is better than them finding out on the news," Billy replied.

"I know, Son, but just make sure you know that some people may think it is kind of sick to find remains," James said.

"Alright, Dad, I will make sure I only talk to the friends that will not feel sick over it. We got a deal?"Billy asked.

"Deal," James replied and started the coffee. He then called work to inform them of what was going on and told them that he was taking the week off of work. Just as he hung up the phone, Courtney and Andy walked into the kitchen.

"Hi, Dad," Andy said.

"Morning, Andy," he replied and went and got out two coffee cup and waited for the coffee to finish brewing as Courtney got the kids ready for school.

Later that day, James was off to the store, leaving Courtney at the house to keep watch. She was sitting on the front porch drinking a cup of tea, waiting for anyone to show up. She sat for a while until she saw a car coming down the road. She could tell it was a police cruiser. She got up from her chair and met the car in the driveway. "Hello, Officer McCabe. What can I do for you?" she asked.

"Well," he began as he got out of his car. "I just wanted to check around a bit. We have discovered that the remains are of a girl named Linda Kelly. She used to live in a little house right over there," he said as he pointed to the right side of the house.

"What are you talking about, a house that was where?' she asked.

"Years ago, there used to be a house that sat right there. This land use to be old farm land, the Kelly's use to work the farm with the Wells. Then one day the whole family disappeared," he stated.

"How does a family disappear?" Courtney asked.

"We just thought that they had a falling out and moved away, but this changed everything," he stated. "So anyway, can I look around on the other side of the house? I am sure that after all these years, there is nothing to find, but I have to check," the officer stated.

"You can look wherever you want. I hope that you can find something to help you," Courtney replied.

Just as the officer was about to go to the other side of the house, James pulled up. James approached the officer to find out what was going on. "Hello," James stated as he put out his hand to shake with the officer.

"Hi, I was just telling your wife that the remains belonged to Linda Kelly, a little girl that lived next door. Your wife was nice enough to let me look around a bit," the officer said.

"That is fine with me, officer. I am going to install an alarm on the trail down to the cave so no one gets down there and disrupts the investigation," James replied.

"Thank you for that. It will help us if the cave stays empty, in case we need to go back there for prints," the officer replied, then walked to the empty lot next to the Stealth home.

James and Courtney took the alarm and the gate down to the corner of their property. Courtney held the alarm while James went back to the garage to get a hammer. When he returned, he hammered the posts for the gate into the ground and set up the gate. The next step was to install the alarm, set the alarm triggers, then made sure that they worked. He climbed over the gate, and as soon as he began to walk the alarm that Courtney was holding began to go off. "Well at least we know it works," Courtney

said as the couple headed back to the house.

Courtney and James met Officer McCabe in the drive way. "There was nothing left in the lot next to your house, just grass," he stated. "I thank you both for being so helpful," he continued. "I wish we had more people like you. Most shut the door in our face or let people trample on a crime scene," Officer McCabe said.

"Well, I guess it is going to sound funny, but I watch the crime shows on television, and I guess that I made sure that we did what the show told us to do," James said as he laughed at himself.

"I think that more people should go by what the television says then," the officer replied and shook James' hand and got in his car. "Be prepared, the media will be calling on you."

"They already have and I will deal with it. You may have to come back to arrest them if they keep bothering us," James stated and smiled at the officer as he backed out of the driveway.

With the officer gone, and the facts out, Courtney began to think about the attic. She wanted so badly to find a picture of the old house that used to stand next door. That must have been the house that Linda used to live in. "James, I need to get back in that attic. I want to find a picture of the house," she said.

"Why do we need a picture of the house? We already have one with Joseph and Rebecca in front of it?" he asked.

"No, not that house, not our house, I want a picture of Linda's house, the Kelly home. I can't explain it, but I think it will help us get Joseph's spirit out of our house," Courtney replied.

"Okay, we can go back to the attic," James said.

CHAPTER

TWELVE

THE ATTIC

(Part three)

This time, Courtney and James were standing at the attic stairs. They were concerned about going up. "James, I can feel that he is here, he is waiting for us," she said.

"It is clear that he is here, but he can't hurt us C.J. He is a ghost. Let's go up," he said and grabbed the pull cord for the stairs.

"I will go first," James said to his wife as he got in front of her and began to climb the stairs. James stood at the top of the stairs. "Are you coming, C.J.?" he then asked.

"Sure am. I just wanted to check on something first," she stated as she tucked Linda's lock of hair into her back pocket and headed to the ladder. She climbed up to the top step and took her husband's hand as he helped her get into the attic. The two of them stood still for a few seconds. "Well, I guess we just start opening boxes," Courtney said to her husband.

"I think you are right" he replied and grabbed a box.

Courtney and James were getting into box after box. Courtney had found a few pictures but not of the whole house. She had a few of the side of a house that was closest to their house. She continued her search until she came across a box full of pictures of the old neighborhood. "James, come check this out!" she yelled.

"What is it?" he replied as he walked over to his wife.

"I found pictures of the old house. Look, it sat right out that window. You would never know by looking now, but it was a cute little house," she stated and handed a picture to her husband.

"So this is where Linda used to live," James stated.

"Yes, from what the officer said," Courtney replied. Just as she was about to get another picture out of the box, the stairs to the attic closed behind them. "James, what the hell just happened? There is no one here but us. Who closed the stairs and how are we getting out?" Courtney asked in a state of panic.

"Hold on," James said and walked to where the trap door was.

He bent down and pushed on the stairs. "I can open it C.J., just hold on," he said and tried. James got his body down as close as he could to the trap door. He pushed with both arms as hard as he could, being careful not to fall forward. He could feel the door begin to open. He then gave it a shove and the steps fell open. He grabbed onto the beam on the left side of the ladder and leaned forward and pushed the folded stairs forward to open them all the way. "There, we are not trapped," he stated and turned toward Courtney. As he did, he began to let go of the beam. He noticed that there was writing on it. "Courtney, this beam says JOSEPH on it."

"What! Let me see," she stated and headed over to where her husband was. "Holy shit, it does. It looks like he carved his name into this beam at some point in time," she said. Then she thought for a second. "James, do you think that this is what Linda wanted us to find?" she asked. She got an answer right away. Not an answer from James, but from Linda herself. Courtney and James were looking at the word JOSEPH carved in the wood when they noticed blood dripping down onto it. "James, where is that blood coming from?' she said and they both looked up at the ceiling of the attic. The couple could see words written on the ceiling. The words read; "You found him, now dig, dig, and dig."

"Where should we dig Linda, where do you want us to dig?" Courtney asked, knowing that it was Linda.

"Please, Linda, we need you to help us!" James yelled and he got to his feet.

"Dig up Joseph," were the next words to appear. "Dig on the blood!" were the next words written on the wall.

"Okay, Linda, what blood?" Where is Joseph's body?" Courtney asked. Then the words rang loud in the attic.

"Get out of my house!" Joseph demanded.

"We are not leaving until we help Linda!" James returned, as the attic window flew open.

"Linda, dig where? Please help us!" Courtney stated. Then Linda let out a scream, and all was quiet. "James, where do we dig? What blood is she talking about?" she asked her husband as she went over and closed the window.

"I don't know. I wish I could figure it out C.J." Then James sat down on one of the chairs that they uncovered. He sat there in silence just thinking about what Linda had written and said. Then he had an idea. "Courtney, could you go down to the garage and get me a hammer and a hand saw?" James asked.

"Sure, but why?" Courtney responded.

"I have an idea; I will tell you when you get back," James replied.

"Okay, I will. I'll be right back," Courtney said.

Courtney climbed down the ladder and into the office. "Hi, Penny," she stated as she headed to the bedroom door. "Penny come," She called realizing that the dog had not been out for a while. She walked down the stairs to the front door, opened it and let the dog out. She then headed to the garage to get what James requested. When finished, she left the garage, making sure she closed and locked the door tightly behind her.

Courtney rushed to the front door of the house with Penny right behind her. Once in the office, Courtney went up the attic stairs and handed James the hammer. Then she set the saw down beside him. "James, will you tell me what you are doing now?" she asked.

"I think that she wanted us to dig where the blood was, and this is where the blood dripped from her words, right on top of Joseph's name," James stated as he grabbed the hammer and began slamming it down on the flooring between the beams.

"I think you have lost your mind! You can't dig here!" Courtney stated. But before she could finish getting her words out, James had found something, something buried between the floor boards of the attic. Courtney stood with her hands on her hips with that "are you out of your mind?" look. She was unaware of what James had found until he showed it to her. "What the hell?" she said. "How did that get there?" she questioned.

"I don't know how it got here, but we need to call the police," James stated as he set the weapon back down not wanting to put prints on it. "Courtney, I think this is the gun that Joseph used to kill Linda," he stated as he reached into his pocket and grabbed his cell phone.

"9-1-1, what is your emergency?"

"My name is James Stealth. My wife and I are the folks that found the remains in the caves. You know, it has been all over the news. Well, I have just found a gun in our attic, trapped between the floor boards. I think it may have been used as the murder weapon. Officer McCabe is the investigator and I think he needs to come see this," James stated.

"Okay, I will send someone right out to check out the gun."

James and Courtney went downstairs to wait for the police to arrive. "James, how do we explain the fact that we ripped up the floor board? It's not like the blood letters are still there."

"Well, I am going to tell them that the stairs closed behind us and I was trying to find a way to get to the other side to pull them down. That is all I can come up with. It's believable, I guess, unless you have something better," he said.

"No, I think that if we tell them the truth, we will both be spending the night in the Mental Health Unit at the hospital for believing in ghosts, and I don't want that," Courtney replied.

In about ten minutes, there was a knock at the door. James was the first one to get up. He opened the door to see Officer McCabe standing there. "I hear you have found something I may want to see," he stated as James waved him to come in. James closed the door behind him and asked him to follow them upstairs. He showed the officer the attic stairs and explained that the gun was at the top of the stairs. He told him the story of how the stairs closed behind them and how they were trying to find their way out. He also told him that he was the only one who touched the gun.

Office McCabe climbed the attic ladder. He pulled himself up and looked down where James had busted through the first layer of flooring. There was a pistol sitting on the beam next to where the hole was. "Okay, I am going to have to call in the crime scene unit. In the meantime, you and your kids are going to have to leave the house until the scene is cleared, maybe overnight," he yelled down the stairs to James and Courtney.

"Alright, officer, we will get a few things together and call a hotel. We don't want to cause any problems with the investigation," James replied as Courtney began grabbing clothes out of the dresser.

"James," Courtney said as she grabbed the suitcase. "What are we going to tell the kids? They are going to find out about this on the news sooner or later and we are going to have to tell them. This is bigger than finding bones in a cave. This is our home," she said with concern in her voice.

"You let me take care of the boys. You just pack and I will call my boss to see if he could take the dog for a few days. You know we will never find a hotel that will take a dog," he stated.

"We could always stay at my mothers or your mothers," Courtney replied.

"C.J., do you really want them to know what is happening here?" he asked.

"No, I guess not," she replied as she headed out of their bedroom and into Billy's room. She was packing pajamas and a change of clothes when she heard Penny begin to bark. "James, what time is it?" she yelled. James looked at his watch; "It's two fifteen, C.J., just like clockwork!" he yelled back and hung up the phone. "C.J., I told my boss about what we found, and he will take the dog!" he yelled from the bedroom as the officer came back downstairs.

"Are you guys set here?" he asked. "I have to escort you out of the house. We have to print and dust the attic and seal off the scene. I really do think it will be a late night, so the hotel is the best option right now," he stated.

"I think that Courtney is just finishing up. Then we will be ready to go outside to wait for our kids to come home from school and we will be out of your way, officer."

Courtney and James met the boys at the bus stop. They watched as the crime scene investigators drove past them down the dirt road. "Mom, what is going on?" Andy asked as they drove away.

"Dad has to talk to you about something" Courtney replied.

"Boys, Mom and I found something in the attic today. The attic door was jammed and I tried to open it and we found a gun," he began.

"A gun?" Billy questioned.

"Yup, a gun, I am not sure why it was up there, but the police are checking it out. We just have to stay at a hotel for one night," James said.

"A hotel, that's awesome," Billy stated.

"What about school tomorrow?" Andy asked.

"You will be going to school tomorrow. Don't even think that you are not going," James stated with a grin.

CHAPTER

THIRTEEN

THE HOTEL

James grabbed the luggage from the truck as Courtney got the key card from the front desk. She met him back at the car and told him what the room number was. She also told the boys there was an indoor pool. The boys were excited because they had never swam in one before and they really wanted too. Once inside the room, James told the boys to pick the bed they wanted to share, and then he would take them swimming. He knew that if he did not take them right away, they were going to drive him crazy until he did. "Court are you coming?" James asked.

"No, I think I better stay here where it is quiet and call both our mothers or they are going to flip a gasket if they hear this on the news," she replied as she grabbed her cell phone.

"All right, but when you are done, come to the pool, or if the boys finish, we will meet you back here and get ready to go to dinner," James stated and closed the door behind him, leaving Courtney to make her calls.

Courtney's first call was to James' mom. She was the one who would really panic if she heard about a gun being found in their attic. "Hello?"

"Hi, it's Courtney, how are you?" she asked.

"I am fine. What's up with the bones you found? I saw that the house was on the news. How come James never called me?" she questioned.

"He didn't? He was supposed to call you. I told him to but then the police came and he may have forgotten. Anyway, I wanted to tell you now that we recently had another development. James and I were in the attic, and the stairs abruptly closed behind us. James tried to cut his way through the floor to get to the other side of the stairs and he found something," Courtney said with a long sigh.

What did he find?" she asked.

"Well, stay calm when I tell you this," she said taking a deep breath. "He found a gun," Courtney said, waiting to see what she was going to hear back.

"What do you mean, he found a gun! What kind of gun? Did anyone get hurt? Did you call the police? What is going on Courtney? How come James didn't call me? Is he all right?" Brenda said in a state of panic and fear.

"Calm down, calm down, James is fine. Everything is fine. The police are at the house taking the gun and I am sure they will fingerprint it. Other than that, we are just staying at the hotel until tomorrow," Courtney said.

"Well, are you sure that James is fine and the kids are fine?' she asked again.

After five minutes of telling her that everyone was fine, Courtney finally hung up the phone. "Now, I have to call my mother," she said out loud and shook her head. "That call can wait until after I take a shower," she said and headed to the bathroom.

Courtney took off her jeans, took the lock of Linda's hair out of her pocket and set it on the sink. She got undressed and climbed into the shower. The hot water felt great on her back. After spending all that time in the attic, she needed to relax. She was washing her hair when all of a sudden she could feel a cold rush come over her. She could see her breath as if it was a cold winter's day. She shuttered from the cold and tried to adjust the water. She could hear the phone ringing in the other room. She just stood in the shower, wondering what was going on. Then the feeling was gone and the water was warm and so was the air. The phone had stopped ringing and things were back to normal. Courtney got out, dried off and went to reach for Linda's hair. She could see that the lock of hair was gone. She felt a feeling of loss come over her, as if someone had died. She opened the bathroom door and looked around for the hair. She turned back and looked at the bathroom floor. "Where is it?" she screamed. "Where did it go?" she yelled. Courtney panicked. She threw the towels around the bathroom.

She ran her hand across the counter by the sink as well as looking in the shower. She was determined to fine that lock of hair. Courtney dropped to her knees and crawled around on the floor. Tears were falling from her eyes and she could barely see. She was so involved in finding the lock of hair that she did not hear James and the boys come in.

"Courtney, what are you doing?" James asked.

"James! Her hair, it's gone; I can't find it anywhere!" Courtney yelled.

"What hair?" James asked.

"Linda's," she replied.

"Okay," James stated and reached down to help his wife stand up. "Courtney, get up. We will find it, but you are out of control right now. Calm yourself down," he said and helped his wife to her feet.

"James, I need that hair! For some reason, it makes me feel closer to Linda," she stated.

"I will find it. You just go get yourself dressed for dinner," James replied.

"James, I…." Courtney started to say.

"Shush," he said and put his finger lightly on her lips. "I will find it. You just calm down and I will find it. It is not like it could disappear!" he stated.

James helped Courtney out of the bathroom and sat her in a chair. He opened her suitcase and took out clothes for her to wear to dinner. He then took a few dollars out of his wallet and gave them to Andy. "Boys, go get a few sodas out of the soda machine while mom gets dressed for dinner."

"But Dad, we haven't changed out of our swim trunks yet," Andy said.

"I know. You can change when you get back. Now, go!" he demanded.

With the boys out of the room, James helped Courtney get dressed. She had tears streaming down her checks.

"James," she said calmly. I need that hair. I think it is helping me to help Linda,"she continued.

"I know, hon. I will find it," he stated, putting her shirt on over her head. "I will not stop looking until I find it. You just sit here and pull yourself together before the kids come back."

James got up and was headed to the bathroom when something caught his eye. He saw a woman, the same woman from one of the pictures that Linda was in. He could see her reflection in the mirror. She was pointing, saying something that James could not hear. He turned to see what she was pointing at. He was looking at the stand that the phone was on, and off to the side of the phone was the lock of Linda's hair. He turned to look back at the mirror, but the image was gone.

"C.J., I found it," he stated as he picked up the hair.

"Oh, thank God!" Courtney exclaimed. "James, I was in the shower and all of a sudden the water got cold. Then the phone rang and when I got out of the shower, her hair had disappeared. I think that Joseph was here. I don't know for sure, but someone was in that bathroom with me," she stated, holding Linda's lock of hair very tightly.

"I believe you. I saw Linda's mom in the mirror. She was pointing to the phone. I think she was telling me where the hair was. It sounds to me like this lock of hair is the link between you and Linda. Maybe even the link to you and the whole family. All I know," he began, but he was cut off by the boys returning from the soda machine.

Courtney tucked Linda's hair in her pocket and went over to the boy's suitcase. She took a deep breath and got clothes out for them.

Billy, Andy, Courtney and James went to a local diner for dinner. The boys were excited because they had not eaten out as a family in a very long time. "Mom, can I have whatever I want?" Billy asked.

"I don't care," was the response she gave him. James added that they could have whatever they wanted, but to make sure they kept room for dessert. He wanted to take the kids to the sundae bar that the hotel offered. He figured that would keep their minds off the fact that they were not able to be at home.

"Are you Courtney and James Stealth?" The couple looked over their shoulders to see a man with a camera crew standing on the right hand side of the table.

"I am James Stealth," James replied and stood up and stood in front of the camera.

"Could you please leave? My family is having dinner right now," James demanded.

"We just wanted an interview about the remains found down by the cave and the weapon found at your house. Do the police think they are connected?" the reporter asked and put the microphone in his face.

"I think it is safe to say that the police are still investigating, and now I want you to leave!" James replied. "If you need help finding the way out, I can call an officer to escort you," he demanded.

"I see you are not ready for an interview, but how about your wife?" the reporter asked.

"I said, leave!" James demanded and grabbed his cell phone from his pocket. "Or I will be forced to call the police," he stated firmly and put his hand in front of the camera. James watched as the reporter gathered up his crew and left the diner obviously disappointed.

"What nerve they have coming here while we are eating!" he stated with discontent as he sat back down.

"Daddy, I wanted to talk to the reporter. I think it would be cool to be on the news," Andy said with a smile.

"It's not cool if the police are investigating a crime and the reporters are reporting the wrong information."

Later that evening, Courtney and James watched the news. The boys were on their bed playing with the Game Boy Billy got for his birthday. James was watching to see what the reporters were going to say about their visit to the restaurant. Surprisingly, there was no report on that. There was, however, a report about the remains that were found. "The remains that were found yesterday down at the old cave that runs behind Beacon Road are the remains of a little girl, Linda Kelly. She was the daughter of Bart and Mary Kelly. She had been reported missing back in the sixties," the reporter stated. "The police are saying that the remains of the skull show that she may have been shot in the head. They are performing an ongoing investigation. At this time, they are investigating a weapon found in the old Wells house. The weapon was found by the same people who found the remains, the Stealth's. At this time, James and Courtney have not made any comment," he said. Then the reporter put up a few pictures of the house and tried to explain where the couple had found the weapon. They reported it was found in the couple's attic, but not mention anything about the floor boards.

"Just like a reporter to mess up the truth. This is why I didn't want to talk to them. They will never get the story straight until they are forced to," James said and then turned the channel to something else.

"I hope we can get back in the house tomorrow," Courtney said to her husband.

"Mom, I miss Penny," Billy said.

"We all do, hon, but she is in good hands and we will see her tomorrow, no matter what."

"I am sure we will be going home in the morning or after you get home from school. Either way, we will be home sometime tomorrow," James responded. "Let me call officer McCabe and see if he has any idea what is going on and when we can get home." James picked up the phone and called the police department. "Can I talk to Officer McCabe please?" James asked.

"He is out on a call. Can I take a message?" the dispatcher asked.

"This is James Stealth. I was just wondering when I can get my family back in the house. Could you please have him call me back when he gets in?" James asked.

"Sure thing, Mr. Stealth," the dispatcher responded. "I will give him the message as soon as I see him."

James said thank you and hung up the phone. "I guess he is out on a case. He is going to call me later," he stated as he put his cell phone back in his pocket. "Why don't the two of you take your shower and get ready for bed. You have school in the morning."

"Okay Dad, I will go first," Andy stated.

"I wanted to go first!" Billy exclaimed.

"Fine, you can go first," Andy said and sat back down on the bed and waited his turn for the shower.

With the boys all tucked in and the television turned down low, the couple was sitting on the bed together whispering about the last few days events. "James, we have to put Linda's remains to rest somehow. That is the only way this will be over. I really believe that if she is put to rest, then Joseph will leave the house. "He will have no reason to stay," she said.

"I think you are correct, but how do we do that? Will the police release her remains from their evidence to bury her?" he asked.

"I think that is what they do. She will be released to family at least that is how I think it works." Courtney replied.

"I just hope she has family. Otherwise, I guess we have to ask if we could give her a burial. Somehow, we have to set her free to go to heaven or she will be stuck here forever, James," Courtney said.

The call came in at about ten pm. "Hello," James said.

"Mr. Stealth, I am sorry to call so late, but they said you wanted to hear from me," Officer McCabe said.

"Yes, I was just wondering how the investigation was going and when we may be able to get back into the house?" James asked.

"We are all set in the house. You can come back at anytime. I am sorry I didn't call you before and tell you. I meant to, but I had another case I had to finish up," the officer stated.

"Thank you, Officer McCabe. I have another question. Did anyone come and claim Linda's remains?" James asked.

"No, I am not sure she has family left," he responded.

"So what will happen to her?" he questioned.

"Well, we have to wait and report the story for about a week. If no one claims her, the county will bury her in the cemetery by the police station. It is quite sad. No one ever comes to visit any of the graves over there. They don't even get a head stone, just a marker with their name," Officer McCabe stated.

"Well, if no one claims her, could we possible bury her in a cemetery of our choice and take responsibility for her grave and her head stone? She deserves a proper burial." James said, looking at Courtney, who face was frozen, waiting for the officer's response.

"I will have to talk to my supervisor, but I am sure as long as it is public record, it would be alright. I will let you know as soon as I find out," the officer said.

"Thanks, officer, I appreciate your help," he stated and hung up the phone.

"Well?" Courtney questioned.

"We will see. We can go home. That is the good news. The other news, about the grave, well we have to wait a week and see if anyone claims her. If not, we can bury her. The officer is not sure he has to talk to his supervisor to approve this," James stated. "Do you want to wake the boys and go home?" James then asked.

"No, let them sleep. They have school tomorrow," Courtney replied.

CHAPTER

FOURTEEN

THE REPORTERS

James and Courtney dropped off the boys at the bus stop and went back to the house. The second they walked in, they could feel cold air drifting in from everywhere. The house itself felt different. It was almost alive. "James, something is wrong in this house. Do you feel it?" Courtney asked.

"I feel it," James answered.

"I think that Joseph is here," Courtney stated. Just as James was about to respond, it started.

The television turned on by itself and there in the television was a man. It was Joseph. He was standing by the edge of a bed in a small child's nursery. They could see that the person on the bed was Linda. She was naked and tears were flowing down her face like water. He was laughing as he touched her unformed breast. He leaned in to kiss her and stopped. He turned to see his wife standing there. Rebecca let out a scream. "Joseph, what are you doing?" she screamed and headed to the phone by the bed.

"I am calling the police!" she yelled.

James and Courtney watch the television in fear as Joseph went to the dresser in his bedroom and grabbed his gun he kept tucked away in the top drawer. He grabbed the trigger tightly, puller it and shot Rebecca as she was picking up the phone on the night stand. Courtney let out a scream and ran to the television. "NO!" she yelled, as James reached to stop her. Just as he caught her, the screen went black. "No!" she screamed and pulled free from her husband. "Why! Why would someone touch a little girl like that?" she said and began to cry uncontrollably on the living room floor. "Why would he kill his own wife?" she continued. James bent down next to his wife. He could feel the cold air rush out of the house and a faint voice saying.

"Now you know." It was not the voice of Joseph, but rather a woman's voice. It was Rebecca who was telling this story. James took Courtney by the hand and helped her to her feet. He then helped her up the stairs to the bathroom. "I am going to draw a bath for you, hon," he stated as he started the water.

"Okay, I think maybe that will calm my nerves. James, make

sure you take Linda's hair with you when I am in the tub; I don't want it to become missing," Courtney said.

"I will," he said and went to the bedroom. He noticed right away that the detectives had been there. The room was a mess, and the dressers had been moved. He took a peek in the office and he could see police had taped over the attic door. The tape read: "POLICE LINE DO NOT CROSS." James shook his head. "Don't have to worry about that," he said and grabbed Courtney's robe and went back into the bathroom. "C.J., the attic is closed off with police tape," he said as he entered the bathroom.

"Really, I guess we are not going back up there," she responded from the tub. "James, could you get me a cup of tea? I just want to relax for a few minutes."

"Sure thing, Hon," he said hearing an alarm going off down by the path to the caves. "Hold on, hon. I have to check the alarm," he said and walked out of the bathroom.

"James, call the cops if someone is down there! James! James, are you listening to me!" Courtney yelled.

James was at the bedroom window. He could see a news van at the side of the road and the reporters heading down the path. "I hear you, Hon! I am calling right now! There are news reporters down by the path!" he yelled as he grabbed his phone.

Courtney got out of her bath and grabbed a towel. She rushed to the bedroom to make sure that James was still there. When she got in the room, James had the window open and he was screaming at the reporters to get off the property. He then yelled that he had called the cops. "James, what should we do?" Courtney asked.

"I already called the cops. I don't want to go out there. Someone may have a gun or something," James replied.

"That is not what I meant. What should we do about this house? I want my life back. I am tired of our lives becoming a freak show for the media," she said with tears in her eyes. "What if the boys were home and outside playing? This has to stop for their sake and ours. James, I want this man arrested so the media will learn to leave us alone."

"Okay Court, I will make sure the officer knows that when he gets here," he replied.

James and Courtney watched as the reporters headed down the path. There was nothing they could do to stop them. They were not going to interfere. If they did, it may cause a problem. The land was clearly posted, and the path was blocked so they were right to call the cops. "C.J., the cop is pulling in now. James left the window in the bedroom and took off down the stairs. He met the officer at the front door.

"I want those reporters arrested!" he demanded.

"Calm down Mr. Stealth. Where are they? I see the van, but not the reporters," the officer asked.

"There are two of them and they are headed down the path," James replied.

"The path is clearly posted!" Courtney added. "We made sure of that and there is a gate and everything!" she demanded.

"Okay, I will go check it out," the officer stated and headed to the path.

Officer McCabe caught up with the reporters heading toward the cave.

"Excuse me, didn't you see the posted signs?" the officer asked.

"We were just trying to get some pictures for our news report," one of the reporters stated.

"Well, the cave is off limits and the trail is posted by the property owner. You need to leave," McCabe stated.

"Why, because we bothered them at dinner last night? We were only trying the get a story when Mr. Stealth really got upset. So we left," the reporter said.

"Really, so you were bothering him at the restaurant?" Officer McCabe questioned.

"Not bothering, just trying to get information," the reporter replied.

"Well, you need to leave here immediately!" McCabe demanded.

"We will as soon as we get our outside shots of the cave," the reporter stated.

"I said now! If you don't, I will arrest you for trespassing and interfering in a crime investigation." Officer McCabe said

forcefully.

"Fine, we will leave," the reporter stated and waved his partner to follow him back up the trail, with officer McCabe right behind them.

The reporters loaded up their equipment while Courtney was yelling from the porch. "I want them arrested for trespassing!" she screamed to the officer.

Officer McCabe approached the porch. "Mrs. Stealth," he stated.

"Call me Courtney," she demanded.

"Courtney, I can't arrest them without giving them a warning," he stated as he stepped onto the porch.

"We have given them a warning. They were here the other day and James asked them to leave," she said pointing at her husband.

"He told them they were not welcome, basically. He said he was not giving them permission to go to the caves and he then refused to talk to them, right hon?" Courtney stated.

"When they came, they asked if they could go to the cave and I said no, and I said I would not give a statement, because I did not want to interfere with your investigation." James stated.

"So they were warned the other day?" McCabe asked.

"Yes," Courtney replied.

"Well, that changes things," he said and headed over to the reporter's van. Along the way, the officer called dispatch to send a second car.

Officer McCabe approached the reporter's van from the driver's side. "Can I see your identifications?" he asked.

"Why do you need that?" one of the reporters asked.

"Just let me see your identification," he stated.

"Okay," he responded and grabbed his wallet out of his pocket. He handed his license to the officer.

"Can you explain to me what is going on?" he asked.

"Well Mr." he began then looked at the identification. "Mr. Ramithol, were you out here the other day?"

"I was, but what does that have to do with anything? He asked.

"Were you and your partner asked to leave the property and denied access to the caves?" he asked.

"Well Officer, we were, but," Officer McCabe grabbed the reporter by the wrist before he could finish his statement. "You are under arrest for trespassing," he stated and asked the man to turn around as he cuffed him. He then went to the other side of the truck where the other reporter was standing, loading up the equipment.

"May I help you officer?" he questioned. "Yes you can. You can hand me your identification." McCabe stated.

"Well," he began, and then stopped.

"You see that cop car pulling down the road?" Officer McCabe asked.

"Yes? What is he here for?" the reporter asked as he began to back away from the officer.

"Don't do anything stupid here. He is here to help me take you and your friend into custody. You were warned the other day to leave the property. So now it is definitely trespassing. Please turn around and put your hands on your head," he said as he put one hand on his gun. He could see that the officer that arrived on the scene had already put the other reporter in custody in the back seat of his car.

With both reporters in custody, all that was left was for the officers to get a tow truck to the scene. Officer McCabe called the tow truck while he had the other officer verify the story with Courtney and James. He had already heard the story, but he wanted to make sure that he had someone else to back it up. Reporter

Ramithol admitted that they had been there the other day. The reporter Brad was sticking to his story. It did not matter to Courtney and James. All they cared about was that they would not be coming back. They were the cop's problem now.

Courtney closed the front door and turned to James. "We have to put this story to a rest. I can't take these crazy reporters coming anymore."

"I know C.J. We just have to wait a few more days to see if a family member comes forth. Then we'll ask if we can claim the remains," James responded. Courtney reached into her front pocket and grabbed the lock of Linda's hair. "I want to bury this with her. I think that I can say goodbye once she is buried," Courtney stated.

"I know you will be able to," James responded and walked over and put his arm around his wife.

"Can I see her hair?" he asked. Courtney had a death grip on the lock of hair.

"James, I need this; I can't explain it, but please be careful with it," she said as she loosened up her grip and gave the hair to her husband.

"I will be careful I promise. I just wanted to see if I could get anything from it, like a vibe, or maybe I would see something," he said and took the lock of hair in his right hand. He closed his eyes and took a deep breath. He held the lock for just about a minute, and nothing happened. He opened his eyes, handed the hair back to his wife. "Well, I guess that didn't do us any good, now did it?" he stated.

Courtney and James decided to get out of the house for a bit. They hooked Penny up to her leash and took her for a walk down the road. They just needed to get some fresh air and tried to take their mind off the fact that they had to wait for the police to tell them if they could have Linda's remains

The wait was killing Courtney inside. She tried to forget, but she wanted Linda to be buried properly and it was something she was not going to be able to let go. "James, what if we can't get her? What if they put her in an unknown grave and she just can't get to heaven? I don't think I could live with myself if that happens," Courtney said.

"C.J., try not to worry about that," he said and stopped with the dog. He turned to his wife, took her by the hand and said, "No matter what happens, I promise you, I will try my best to make this right for her. That little girl deserves to go to heaven," he stated with conviction.

"I know, but," she began to say, but something stopped her. She could feel a sense that something was about to change everything.

"James, check your phone," she said as if she was questioning whether it was going to ring or not. James reached into his pocket, took out his phone just as it began to ring.

"Hello?" he said. "This is he," he continued. "Yes, I was," he said and looked at his wife. "Really, are you sure?' he said and smiled at his wife. "Okay, sir, please let us know for sure as soon as you can, and thank you, thank you so much," he said ending his conversation.

"What is it, James?" Courtney demanded. "Who was that? What did they say?"

"Well, that was the Chief of Police. He asked if we were interested in burying the body because Officer McCabe said we would be. He also said that if no one claims her by Friday, we can have the remains to bury her wherever we want, as long as we let them know where we'd bury her. He wants to make sure it is public record just in case a family member comes forth later." Courtney wrapped her arms around her husband's neck and cried tears of joy.

"I hope to God that we get to bury her James. I think she needs us to do that," she stated, then let go of her husband's neck.

"She does need us, C.J. She has since the day we moved in," James replied.

CHAPTER

FIFTEEN
(The final goodbye)
THE BURIAL

It was Thursday, just about noon, when the phone rang. "Hello," Courtney said as she put the phone to her ear.

"Hi, is this the Stealth residence?"

"Yes it is; I am Courtney Stealth," she responded.

"My name is Jack. I run the records department at the Salem Police Department. I am calling to inform you that Officer McCabe will be releasing the remains of Linda Kelly tomorrow. He wanted me to call you to tell you that if you wanted the remains, you could come get them tomorrow at ten thirty am. Otherwise, he will release them to the county for burial."

"Thank you for calling. We will be there to get them. Is there a special door for evidence release?" she asked.

"If you pull in the parking lot, it is the door on the left side of the building. You go down the flight of stairs and to the right and you will see the sign for evidence holding. I will be there. Just ring the bell, show me your identification, and I will release the remains to you," James stated.

"Okay, thank you so much. We will see you tomorrow," Courtney stated and hung up the phone.

Courtney walked out the front door. She yelled to James, who was mowing the lawn. "James!" she screamed and ran toward him, waving her hands in the air to get him to stop the mower.

"What is it, C.J.?" he asked and shut off the mower.

"We got her!" she exclaimed. "We get to pick up the bones tomorrow. We get to bury her!"

"That's the best news, Hon. Now what?" James asked.

"I wanted to know if you would go with me to pick out a headstone. It takes a few weeks to make them, and I want to get started on it so she won't have to wait long," she said,

"Let me finish the lawn. Then we will wait for the boys and we can go as a family," he said. "If that is okay with you."

"Thank you, thank you, thank you!" Courtney yelled and hugged her husband. "I am going to change my clothes and get ready," she said and turned and ran to the house.

Courtney ran upstairs into her bedroom. She got out a clean pair of dress pants and a blouse from her closet. She decided to take a shower. She wanted everything to be perfect today. She walked into the bathroom and turned on the water. She took the lock of Linda's hair out of her jeans, put it in her slacks pocket and set her jeans on the counter by the sink. "I am going to make this right for you, Linda," she said out loud. As she got ready to get in the shower, she could hear a voice in the distance. She could not make it out, but she did not have to. She knew in her heart that it was Linda talking to her. "I can't here you, but I am sure that you are happy to know that I am helping you," she responded and climbed into the shower.

When Courtney got out of the shower, she went downstairs. She could see James sitting on the couch. "James, we need to call some cemetery. We need to find one that we can get Linda into. It has to be a nice one, too" she stated and sat down next to James.

"I already called a few. It looks like we can get her into the Country Side Cemetery. We have an appointment at three pm., so once the boys get home, we can look at it and pick out the stone of your choice," James replied.

"Thanks, James" Courtney replied and hugged her husband.

A few hours later, the boys were home. Courtney explained that they were going to check out a cemetery and purchase a headstone for the little girl whose bones they found. She told them that the deceased girl did not have any family, and that mom and dad wanted to do something nice for her. She also told them that if they didn't do this, she would be buried in an unmarked grave and no one would know about her. "We just don't want her to end up in a place where she can't be found if family does show up," Courtney said. "Do you guys understand what I am telling you?" Courtney asked.

"I think so," Andy responded and waited to hear what Billy had to say.

"I think you are doing something really nice Mommy. If you and Dad did not do this, I would be sad for her," Billy said.

The family and the dog jumped into the truck. They were off to see the cemetery. Courtney was holding her hand over her pocket. She was anxious to see where the final resting place for Linda would be. She watched as James pulled into the cemetery. She could see that it was beautifully maintained. It was freshly mowed with flowers planted everywhere. James pulled up to the front door. He parked the truck and looked at Courtney. "Ready?" he asked.

"Ready as I will ever be," she responded.

"Let's go, boys," James said and waited for them to get out of the truck. The family walked up to the front door. Courtney was holding Billy's hand as James opened the door.

Inside, the family met the cemetery manager.

"Hi" he said and reached out his hand to James. "My name is William. I am the one you spoke with on the phone. You must be James," he said and shook James' hand. "And you must be Courtney," he said and reached out and shook her hand. "If you will follow me, I will show you a few plots that are available that I think you may like. We will start over by the oak tree and go from there," he said and held the door open for the family. He was carrying paper with what Courtney believed was a list of vacant plots. "This first one is my favorite for a single plot," he said and walked toward the tree. There is a couple that is buried near here, but there is one vacant plot and I think it is beautiful," he continued.

Courtney was looking around. She was amazed at how clean and well maintained the area was. She watched as he took them to a plot in the back corner of the cemetery. She was smiling from ear to ear when he pointed to the plot. He began to talk about the cemetery and all the options they would have when Courtney suddenly cut him off.

"This is perfect for her. This plot is so nice and it is a beautiful area," Courtney said. "James, I want to bury her here, please. We will take this plot," Courtney said and looked at her husband to wait for his response.

"Okay, if this is what you want," James said.

"This is what she needs," Courtney responded. "I can feel it, James. This is the spot."

Courtney and James went back to the main building. James went over the paperwork and they signed the necessary papers. "Thank you so much. This plot will be perfect for her," Courtney said.

"You are very welcome. I will make sure that it is dug and ready for tomorrow.

"Will there be a vault or an urn?"

"We are getting her a casket, so I guess a vault, right James?" Courtney asked.

"Most definitely, she deserves a casket," James replied.

The next step was the headstone. James and the family pulled into the parking lot of "Special Monuments." They could see all kinds of display models in the yard. Courtney was the first one to get out of the truck. She walked over to the stones with James and the boy's right behind her. She wanted to pick out the perfect stone. She put her hand in her pocket and found the stone she wanted. It was black and looked like solid marble. She could picture Linda's name written on the front of it. The display model had a picture of a man etched in it. She was hoping that she would be able to do that for Linda.

"Hi, may I help you?" a man asked as he approached.

"Hi, my name is Courtney. This is James, Billy, and Andy. We want to purchase this stone, but I have a question to ask."

"Okay, my name is Edgar Murphy. I am sure I can answer your question," he responded as he shook hands with the family members.

"I just wanted to know if I would be able to put a picture on this stone like the display model, and if it would wear off in time?" she asked.

"This is granite, this is the hardest stone we sell. It is also the most popular because it lasts longer than any other stone we sell. It is the most expensive, but you only have to purchase it once," he said.

"I am not worried about the price," James stated and put his hand on his wife's shoulder. "What do you require for a picture and how long does it take to make the stone?" he asked.

"Well, I need a picture that is at least four by six or bigger. Then I need to know what you want written on it. Takes about a week to ten days to get it made and we deliver it to the grave sight," he said as Courtney looked at James,

"I want this stone," she said.

"Okay, let's go in and do the paperwork. All I need is a down payment right now. You will need to get me the picture and write up what you want on the stone. Just come back with those items for me. The down payment for this stone is $1000.00," he stated and looked at James.

"That's fine," James replied. "I just have to get the checkbook out of the truck. Can I put the rest on a credit card when we come back?" he asked.

"That's fine with me. I am not busy right now so I could have the stone done in less than a week. I just have to sketch out the design from the picture," Edgar stated as they walked into the main building. The family looked around at stones that were set aside for other families. They had identification on them. Billy was very inquisitive and looked at every stone. Andy, on the other hand, wanted nothing to do with it. He sat in the chair by the desk and waited for the paper work to be completed. He was not having a good time with any of this.

With the down payment made, the family went back to town. They stopped at the local diner and grabbed a bite to eat. James looked in the phone book for funeral homes. "We need to get her a casket, and I think we will have to wait until tomorrow, because it is after five."

"We can go look in the morning, before we get her remains. That way the boys will be at school and they don't have to do endure that part. "Thank you, Mom," Andy replied. "I think that part is creepy. I don't mind going to a funeral home, but to pick a casket, no way." Billy on the other hand was fascinated by the whole idea. He begged his father and mother to let him stay home from school and go with them, but they said no. They needed to do this on their own. Besides, school came first.

Friday morning at eight thirty am., both boys went off to school. Courtney had just gotten out of the shower and James had called several funeral homes. He found two that he thought that seemed reputable. The first one was only about five minutes from their house. The second was on the other side of town. The couple got Penny on her leash and headed toward the door. James tried to open it, but it would not budge."C.J., the door is stuck," he said.

"James, turn around. It's not stuck, we are," she said.

James turned around and looked at his wife. "What are you…?" he began, and then realized what his wife was talking about. There was writing on the wall again. It said "No rest for Linda" in crimson red blood. "You can't keep us here, Joseph!" James screamed. "We will get out of here and we will take care of Linda!" he continued to scream and grabbed one of the dining room chairs and threw it through one of the living room windows. As he did this, Joseph let out a scream, a scream that sounded like the word "NO!"

"You can't stop us!" Courtney yelled as she climbed through the window. James picked up Penny and put her through the window and followed her through. Joseph was tossing things around in the house, screaming for James and Courtney to come back. He could not let go of Linda. He needed her in order for him to stay in that house.

Courtney and James jumped in the car with Penny who was barking madly at the house. They began driving down the road and watched as the windows on their house exploded from the inside out. Courtney covered her ears and screamed at the sight of her home being terrorized by the spirit of Joseph Wells. "James, we need to bury her today. Otherwise, we are not going to have a house left!"

"We will get Linda buried today. I promise you that!" James stated with conviction as he sped down the dirt road.

"There is no way I am letting that man further destroy our home!" James stated loudly.

"I know that. Please, James, slow down," Courtney said calmly as to not make things worse.

"Okay, I'm sorry. I just want this to be over. I want that man out of our house!"he stated with demand. "I know, but I also want us to stay alive so just slow down."

James and Courtney arrived at the Berkley Funeral Home. It was a lovely building made of brick. You could tell that it was old, but it was very well maintained. Courtney and James got out of the truck and walked hand in hand to the front door. They rang the doorbell and waited for the funeral director to come to the door. He was a short man. He had dark glasses and he was wearing a suit. "Good morning," he stated as he opened the door. "May I help you?" he asked.

"We need to purchase a casket. We don't want a whole service with a wake and all. We want just a small service for our family," James stated.

"A private service is not very common, but it can be done. Come on in. We can go over the details," he said and then offered his hand to James. "My name is Floyd, Floyd Derek. My father and I run this place by ourselves. We have been in business for many years," he continued as the couple followed him inside. "This is the showing room. This is where we can set up the service that you want. Are you going to have an obituary written?" He asked looking at the couple.

"No, I think it is best if we don't," Courtney replied. It is for the little girl that was found in a cave off of Beacon Road.

"Are you the Stealth's?" Floyd asked.

"Yes, yes we are," James replied.

"We are not looking to make a big deal about this. We just want a private service for her. The media doesn't even know she is being released to us and we want to keep it that way," Courtney said.

"I understand. You don't need to have a media circus here. This is the casket room," he stated and opened the door.

The casket room was a large room. It was filled with caskets of all kinds. There were wooden ones and metal ones and even a few copper ones. Courtney walked in and took James by the hand. "It has to be perfect, James," she stated.

"I think I have one in mind for you," Floyd said. "If you could just follow me, we have another area with caskets for children. I know it is not something most people think of, but kid's caskets are different than adults," Floyd said as he walked around the corner.

Floyd pointed to a casket that had teddy bears on it. It was solid oak and covered with little trees. Courtney looked right past it and saw the perfect casket for Linda.

"No offense, Floyd. I like this one, but I love that one," she said and walked over to another casket.

The casket was made of oak, but this one, this one was perfect for a little girl. The design on this one had little roses carved in the top of the casket. The inside was a light rose color, almost a pink, but not quite. "James, what do you think?" she asked.

"If this is the one that you want, this is the one we will get," James replied.

"Okay, the cemetery said something about needing a vault?" Courtney asked.

"A vault is to protect the casket. It is almost mandatory these days. There are several different kinds, but they all serve the same purpose. They are solid steel and they protect the casket. I can show you a few, or you can just get the cheapest if you want to.

Courtney looked at James. "I think you can just pick the one that you think we need. It doesn't sound as important as the casket."

"Alright, let me get the order form and we can write up what you want for a service and get things ready" Floyd said and walked to his office to get his invoice book. A few seconds later, Floyd emerged from his office with a book in hand. "Okay, when do you think you want the service and where are we taking her to her final resting place? he asked.

"Well we would like to drop her remains off in an hour and have the service around four o'clock if possible," Courtney stated.

"An hour? That's rather sudden, but I guess that would be fine. "Where is her final resting place?" he asked again.

"Country Side," Courtney stated.

"After we get this all set," he said, pointing to his paperwork. "I will give them a call and let them know what time we will be coming for her final service. Do you have someone to say the eulogy?" he asked.

Courtney and James looked at each other. "I will say the eulogy," Courtney said.

"All that is left is the paperwork," Floyd said as he waved them to follow him to the little room next to the casket room.

Floyd and the couple sat down at the table. They talked about the prices of the casket and the vault that they picked out. They signed the contract saying that Courtney and James would pay for all the expenses and James gave him his credit card. "Well, we are all set. Just bring the remains to me and I will get her all ready for you for four o'clock today," Floyd stated.

"Thank you so much," Courtney said and James shook the man's hand. The couple drove to the police station. They arrived at the desk in front of a wall that looked like the front of a jail cell. It was barred up with a key lock on the front of it. "Hello," James called.

"I'm in the evidence room, I'll be right there," a voice answered from another room. "Are you here for the remains?" the clerk called out.

"Yes, I'm James and this is my wife Courtney," James answered. The couple watched as a tall thin man approached from around the corner. He was carrying a small cardboard box. Courtney's heart felt like it could fall to the floor. She knew now that this was real. Linda was really dead. For some reason, she did not connect it the first time they found her bones. But now, she needed to bury her and THAT was real. The clerk took the box and set it down. He took the key out of his pocket, reached through the bars and unlocked the gate. He picked the box up and carried it to the desk. "I take it you are the Stealth's," he said and shook James' hand.

"Yes we are," James replied.

"All I need is some form of identification from one of you and a signature and she is all yours," he stated as he got out the log book.

James took out his wallet. "No," Courtney said as she put her hand on James' wallet. "I have to do this," she stated and reached into her purse. She took out her license and handed it to the clerk. "Just sign here and I will make a copy of your identification and you will be all set."

When the clerk returned, he handed the identification back to Courtney. He checked to make sure that she signed the log, handed over the box and wished them luck. He then opened the gate with the key again, turned and locked it behind him and disappeared down the walkway between stacks of boxed evidence. Courtney took a deep breath. She picked up the box and carried it back up the stairs to the car. James opened the back door so she could put Linda's remains on the seat. The two of them got back into the car and drove back to the funeral home. James waited in the car while Courtney took the box up to the front door. He watched as the

funeral director came to the door and grabbed the box and went back inside. Courtney then returned to the car and the couple headed back toward the house.

James parked the car and let Penny out. She took off, running in the yard. She was happy to be out of the vehicle. James just stood and watched as she ran. He didn't know what he was going to do about all the broken glass, or how he was going to explain it to the boys, but he would come up with something. Courtney picked up the boys at the bus stop. She was not going to even try to explain the broken glass from the windows. She drove into the driveway with the boys who were already asking questions about the glass. "Mom, what happened to the windows?" Andy asked.

"I am not sure, Hon. let's go ask Dad," Courtney said.

The boys entered the house and they were met at the front door by their dad. "Hi, guys. I am sure you are wondering what happened here with the windows, and I really don't know. I think there must have been a gas leak or something that caused the windows to explode, but I am not sure. All I know is there is no problem now, so everything is fine," James stated, hoping the boys would not be very inquisitive. Billy thought about it for a second.

"Shouldn't we call the fire marshal or something if there was a gas leak?" Billy asked.

"If we smell gas, I will call, but for now, I think we are safe," James replied.

With the boys believing what James said, Courtney asked them to get dressed for the funeral. She sent them upstairs to take showers and put on dress pants. The boys fussed for a few seconds, then realized that it would not do them any good. They both took off up the stairs and got themselves ready to go.

The family was dressed and ready to go. Courtney had the lock of Linda's hair securely in her hand. She was not taking any chance of losing it before they got to the cemetery. They all got in Courtney's car and called Penny to come. They did not want to leave her behind, just in case Joseph was still causing havoc. With seat belts locked, the family was on their way to put Linda to rest.

James drove the car into the same parking lot where he and Courtney parked earlier that day. They got the boys out and went to the front door. Floyd was standing in the doorway. "I have been waiting for you," he said. "Come on in. The casket is all set and ready to go," he said and showed the family to the casket. Billy took his mother's hand and walked up to the casket with her. Andy, on the other hand refused to go to the casket. He stayed back with his father and waited for it to be over. Floyd approached Courtney and asked if she wanted to say the eulogy here or at the cemetery.

"I think I will wait until we get to the cemetery to say my goodbye to her," she stated and touched the top of the casket. She then turned to look to the back of the room where James was standing. "Do you need to come up here?" she asked.

"No, I think that I will just stay here with Andy if that is okay with you."

"That's fine, hon. Floyd; I think we are ready to go to the cemetery."

Courtney and the family got into the car and waited for the funeral director and a few workers to load up the casket in the hearse. They followed them down the road to the cemetery. They watched as the men unloaded the casket and placed it on the poles and the canvas over the grave. The family then got out of the car and headed over to the grave. Andy was kind of dragging his feet. He stayed back as far as he could until his father came and took his hand. He reassured him that it was just bones in a box. There was nothing here that could hurt him. Even with the encouraging words from his father, Andy felt very uncomfortable at the cemetery. Courtney turned her attention to her oldest son. "Andy, if you want to stay in the car, that is fine," she said walking toward him. She met her son about halfway to the grave. "I meant it, hon, if you want to go to the car, it is alright." Andy hugged his mother.

"Thank you so much for understanding, Mom, I just don't like cemeteries, I guess," he said and ran back to the car.

Courtney stood next to the casket. She took a deep breath and began to talk. "Well, let's see. All I can say is that this little girl needs to be put to rest. She led a very rough life and she died in a horrible manner. I want to set her free so she can go to heaven to be with her family. I will miss you, Linda, but you are free," she said as she tossed the lock of hair into the grave. Courtney then took a step back and watched as this beautiful ray of light came down over the casket. She could actually see the spirit of Linda rise into the air. "James, do you see this?" she exclaimed.

James, Billy and Courtney watched as Linda's spirit rose up high over the casket. "Thank you, Courtney," she said with a smile on her face. She was dressed in the same dress that Courtney always saw her in, but this time the dress was clean and new. Her shoes were bright and shiny. She drifted off into the air and she was gone.

"We did it, James!" she exclaimed and jumped into her husband's arms. "We did it. She is free!" she said again and began to cry tears of joy.

"You did it, C.J. This was a little girl who asked you for help." The couple started to walk away from the grave. "Billy, are you coming?" Courtney asked.

"Yeah, I was just reading the names on these headstones over here," he responded. "This couple was old when they died. Mom this man was born in January of 1879 and died in July of 1969. That would make him ninety when he died and his wife was born in 1893 and died in July of 1969, as well."

Courtney walked over to where Billy was reading the headstones. She was shocked when she saw the faces that were engraved in the stone. "James, check this out," she stated. "Their names are Sadie and Jeremiah Kelly. This can't be! They were our realtors. How is this possible?" They couldn't have died in the late sixties," she said. James walked over to the headstones.

"Holy shit, not only are they the realtors, but did you notice their last name? They are related to Linda, C.J. The realtors were ghosts. They set us up from the beginning to find Linda." Courtney knelt down next to the headstones.

"Thank you," she whispered and then got back to her feet and walked hand in hand with her husband back to the car. They knew now that the house, the Wells house, was now in their complete possession.

CHAPTER
SIXTEEN
(Home)

James parked in the driveway. He walked around the car and met his wife on the other side of the vehicle. Courtney took a deep breath and smiled at James. "James," she stated.

"What C.J.," he replied.

"We are home. For the first time since we bought this house, it is our home," she stated.

"Yes it is," James replied as he took his wife by the hand.

Courtney and James walked hand in hand to the front door with Andy, Billy, and Penny, right behind them. James took the key out of his pocket and unlocked the front door. "Boys, there is a lot of cleanup work that has to be done so be careful going inside," he said.

"We will, Dad," Billy replied as he waited anxiously until the door opened. Once inside the house the family just stood there. They were unsure of what they were seeing. The house was just the way it was before Joseph made a mess of things. "James, I don't understand?" C.J. Questioned. Courtney and James stood next to the boys in shock. There were letters appearing on the wall. This time they were not in crimson blood color. They were in a beautiful shade of pink. Courtney and her family read the words as they appeared. "THANK YOU FOR HELPING ME TO FIND THE WAY HOME. IT IS BEAUTIFUL HERE IN HEAVEN. I AM FINALLY WITH MY FAMILY." "Mom is that Linda?"

Andy asked looking at the wall. As Courtney began to respond to her son the letters disappeared.

"It sure was," she stated as a tear trickled down her left cheek. This tear was not for a little girl who was lost in the shadows of their "home." This tear was for a little girl who finally found happiness. This single tear was shed for Linda Kelly, a child who found her family. "God bless you Linda," Courtney said as she put her arm around Andy. "We will miss you." At that point Courtney and her family knew that Linda had found happiness, true happiness. Linda had found her way "home."

www.ingramcontent.com/pod-product-compliance
Lightning Source LLC
Chambersburg PA
CBHW070842120626
46556CB00002B/845